GUILTY
CONSCIENCES

Copyright Information

GUILTY
CONSCIENCES

A Crime Writers' Association Anthology

Edited by Martin Edwards

severn
House

This first world edition published 2011
in Great Britain and in the USA by
SEVERN HOUSE PUBLISHERS LTD of
9–15 High Street, Sutton, Surrey, England, SM1 1DF.
Trade paperback edition first published
in Great Britain and the USA 2011 by
SEVERN HOUSE PUBLISHERS LTD .

British Library Cataloguing in Publication Data

Guilty consciences: an anthology of original stories from
    members of the Crime Writers' Association.
    1. Detective and mystery stories, English.
    I. Edwards, Martin, 1955- II. Crime Writers' Association
    (Great Britain)
    823'.0872080914-dc22

ISBN-13: 978-0-7278-8024-6   (cased)
ISBN-13: 978-1-84751-404-2   (trade paper)

Typeset by Palimpsest Book Production Ltd.,
Falkirk, Stirlingshire, Scotland.
Printed and bound in Great Britain by the
MPG Books Group, Bodmin, Cornwall.

CONTENTS

FOREWORD

Various people, including Abraham Lincoln, Benjamin Franklin and Blaise Pascal are credited with the immortal words: '*I am sorry I wrote you such a long letter; if I'd had more time, I would have written a much shorter one.*'

This is the mantra that every writer should have repeating over and over inside their head, along with that invaluable truism, *Less is more.*

Good writing is about firing the reader's imagination with as few words as possible, not describing something in such elaborate detail that the reader feels exhausted and swamped, as if buried beneath a collapsed pallet of remaindered thesauruses. That is something I love about the short story genre: there is little room for elaborate description, as you will see in some of the brilliant works in this gem of a collection.

Guilty consciences? The contributing authors here? Moi included? Guilty about writing such long stories when they could have been so much shorter? I don't think so. Each of these is a tight, sharp, delight.

I believe the short story is long overdue for a renaissance, and the ideal literary form for our increasingly busy, time-poor modern lives. What better for a quick read between tube station stops, or using your e-reader to turn a tedious airport security queue into fifteen minutes of surprises and delight?

Enough said! I would hate to be accused of rambling. Or to have to explain to you that if I'd had more time . . .

INTRODUCTION

Following the successful publication of *Original Sins* last year, it gives me great pleasure to welcome readers to *Guilty Consciences*, the latest anthology of fiction by members of the Crime Writers' Association. And I am delighted that the book is again published by Severn House, whose list now includes many distinguished crime writers, including a number of the contributors whose work features in this collection.

The stories offer many different takes on the theme of guilty consciences, and the contributors are a varied, as well as highly talented, bunch. Two of them – Bob Barnard and the late Harry Keating – earned the genre's highest accolade, the CWA Cartier Diamond Dagger, Ann Cleeves currently has a very successful TV series, *Vera*, based on her novels, and Peter James is pretty much a fixture in the bestselling lists. But apart from these stellar names, I have been keen to include stories written by several of the most gifted members of the new generation of crime writers, such as Dan Waddell, Len Tyler, Bernie Crosthwaite and Claire Seeber. All the contributions have been written specially for this volume, with one particular exception.

Harry Keating, amongst many other achievements during a long and illustrious career as a crime writer and critic, chaired the CWA and edited two of its anthologies; following his death earlier this year, I thought it would be fitting to include a story by him. His widow, Sheila Mitchell, responded very positively, and identified 'The Visitor' as highly suitable for inclusion in this particular book, and was even kind enough to retype the manuscript. This story, which features Harry's most famous character, Inspector Ghote, has only previously appeared in a Penguin India collection, thirteen years ago. It is a characteristically original tale, and readers should bear in mind that Harry's first two names were Henry Reymond. I hope that the appearance of 'The Visitor' is a suitable tribute to a writer of great distinction who showed many personal kindnesses to a host of colleagues in the literary world over the years.

Peter James is Harry's latest successor as chair of the CWA and I am grateful that he has found time in his busy schedule not only to write a foreword to this book but also to contribute a story. My thanks also go to Sheila and all the contributors for their cooperation and patience whilst the book was put together, as well as to the team at Severn House for all their hard work on production and marketing.

Martin Edwards

JUST POPPED IN
Robert Barnard

Robert Barnard received the CWA Cartier Diamond Dagger in recognition of his sustained and outstanding contribution to crime writing over many years. In addition to his many novels and short stories, his publications include an acclaimed study of the work of Agatha Christie.

'What do you think you're doing?' said Claudia. The voice was standard middle class with no genteel aggression to it. On the sofa the black youth looked up from the TV zapper and then back again to it. Not even a smile at Claudia.

'I thought you'd be pleased,' he said finally.

'I probably will be when I've absorbed the shock. You shouldn't go around taking over other people's houses. Breaking in, I call it.'

'Do you? Well you shouldn't. I just popped in. I let myself in with a key.'

'Your old key. I forgot all about that. You didn't have the courtesy to leave it behind when you left.'

'There were lots of kids around with keys. I forget who you were fostering then. Kylie, Ben "call me Benjamin" and – who else? – Alfons. Did you ever find out whether that really was his name?'

'Alfonso. It sounds perfectly normal in Spanish. Can't you stop fiddling with that thing?'

'With wh—? Oh, the zapper. Sure.'

He put it on the coffee table in front of him, but he occasionally cast longing glances at it, as if he yearned for normality to be resumed. Claudia's gaze at him was cooler. Nice build, her eyes said: workouts at gyms, but only occasional, not long daily schedules or anything like that. No absurd biceps, but she approved of his sturdy legs under the worn denim of his trousers. His face – generally amiable and almost inviting, as Claudia vividly remembered. Less genial now, though.

'Do you have a room or a flatlet – somewhere to live?' asked Claudia.

'I moved back with my mother,' said the black boy.

'Good God, Graham,' said Claudia, genuinely concerned. 'Is that wise? Your mother was the reason you were here.'

'Don't I know it. You never knew the half of it. My mother's got breast cancer. She hasn't got the upper hand any longer. I do what I think is right, and she has to conform. The balance of power has shifted completely. I'm boss. I've got the upper hand.'

Claudia's voice took on a schoolmistressy tinge. 'I wasn't thinking of who's physically the more powerful. Your mum had the upper hand because she was mentally stronger, more ruthless, more able to hurt you. That was her strength.'

'*Was*,' said Graham.

'I've known lots of people who suddenly took over – or thought they would – when the partner became ill. It never worked out as they wanted it to. They just became slaves to the incurable one, and for the rest of their lives as often as not. You're either the dominant partner or you're not.'

'And you think I'm not?' said Graham, with a bleak smile.

'I know you're not.'

'You know so little. You don't know what lay behind what happened in this house.'

Claudia left a few moments' silence. 'Could you do with a cup of tea?'

'Yeah . . . Got any of those cookies you used to bake?'

'I've always got some . . . When did you learn to say "cookies"?'

'The US of A – where else?'

'What were you doing there?'

'With a band. They thought it a real sensation having a black English band.'

'Are you still playing?'

'No. We went the way of all bands. But it was nice while it lasted.'

She came through from the kitchen with a plateful of pallid biscuits. 'Harry liked my oatmeal cakes as well.'

Graham kept silent, but his mouth twisted into a derisory smile.

'You can sneer, but it was Harry's salary that made this place possible. That and his organizational abilities. You'd have had a far inferior foster home without Harry.'

'You think so? Didn't strike me like that. He never was quite sure of anyone's name.'

'Well there was a lot of coming and going – that's in the nature of fostering.'

'I know it was. But how do you think it went down with kids from normal backgrounds? "His Dad doesn't even know his name".'

'You could have done worse. Far worse,' said Claudia obstinately. 'And you managed to take advantage of Harry's absence.'

'Oh, I did . . . Still as good as they always were, these oatcakes. Harry was right.'

'He usually was . . . I miss him dreadfully.'

Graham began a sardonic smile at this false feeling, but changed it hurriedly to a gaze of sympathy.

'Long marriages always leave one at the end to loneliness, I suppose. And you had the children as well.'

'Yes,' said Claudia, schoolmistressy again.

'Did the authorities put a stop to that when Harry died?'

'Not exactly. I expect it would have dwindled and stopped when they faced up to the fact that there was no father figure in the household. The ones left began to get a bit unruly. I could have faced it, developed a long-term strategy, but I suddenly decided I didn't want it any more. Can you understand that?'

'Oh, I can . . .' He waved an arm at her. 'I used to love those cups and saucers. And the contents – the typically English tea. I decided to have nothing but Wedgwood when I was grown up, and rich and famous.'

'And have you done just that?'

'No. I forgot about it.' They laughed. 'Children's dreams sound silly when they come from adults.'

'Yes. They reject their early decisions, and that's perfectly natural.'

'Though some of my dreams are still the same as when I was young . . . really young. You know, I think I was unfair to Harry just now.'

'You were. Totally. He kept the place going.'

'Maybe. I was just thinking about our names. That he didn't know their names. It was just that he never used them. And he brushed them aside if anyone insisted on telling him their name. He had pet names for everyone, and that was what he used. Some of them have just come back to me. Kylie. That was "Shyly". Harry didn't really go for shyness, did he? It didn't attract him, not one bit.'

'He had his preferences just as all the foster parents did. It was natural.'

'Maybe . . . yes, I suppose so.'

'But he rejected nobody. All sorts of behaviour and preferences he could turn . . . he could understand and accept.'

'Good old Harry. That was very useful to you.'

'To us. Don't put blame all on one side.'

'Oh, I don't. That would have put the credit all on one side as well, and I wouldn't want that . . . you didn't keep the authorities happy, did you?'

Claudia shrugged. 'We – you and I – were normal people, an unusual couple. Relations like that are more common in central Europe than in dear old England. Or were at that time. The mature woman and the young chap exploring possibilities.'

'*Der Rosenkavalier*,' said Graham.

'Is that that opera?' asked Claudia.

'I went to see it once in Chicago – enormous orchestra, three big soprano voices. It was like living off Black Forest gateau. I came away after two acts. You're bound to get sick if you like a diet of chocolate and cream and super-sweet fruit.'

'I'm sure. But it was never like that, was it? You weren't like that, and neither was I. Always a dash of lemon juice or Fino sherry.'

'If you say so. It all seemed pretty sweet and sickly to a

sixteen-year-old released from the control of school or college. Though of course there was more than a touch of the school-marm in you.'

'Maybe. Not a bad thing either . . . want some more tea?'

Claudia made noises in the kitchen and came back with a fresh pot.

She opened her mouth but Graham got in first.

'We didn't mention Corny.'

Claudia put down the tray carefully. 'Should we have?'

'I think so. Today is the anniversary of her death.'

'Oh, is it? She did all right in her way. Corny Turner, and the all-girl band. They never recovered from her suicide. She was the one who had talent. I think she'd say she had a pretty good life.'

'Oh, you would, would you? I can't say I would. I'd say she was one of those the world does nothing for.'

'What nonsense,' said Claudia briskly. 'She was here for eighteen months. You'd know that. When her band – whatever you call that odd mixture of instruments – started getting engagements we suggested she go – too disturbing to a houseful of difficult children. She represented something they could aspire to but never attain. She was OK about it. Said she'd been wondering whether the time had come to leave.'

'So she went out into the big wide world and made a life with her fellow "musicians" and their pretty-boy hangers-on.'

'Was it so bad? You could have been one, but you never cared for the life there.'

'I was one of the hangers-on; but no – I didn't care for the life. That's been my drawback. I never found a way of life I cared for.'

'You were never one of the hangers-on. You had . . . other interests.'

'So the other interest thought.'

'She didn't think – she knew. And Corny barely looked at you.'

'I never suggested she was smitten. I was sixteen, she eighteen. She liked the experienced sort.'

'Drink up your tea. It'll be cold.'

'Experienced, like Harry.'

'Now you are being silly . . . One thing I always tried to do was take on only girls who would look ridiculous walking down a street with a respectable middle-aged man. Cornelia was the archetypal rock teenager.'

'Oh, hark at her. Archetypal! So what about you then? How come you could walk down a street with a handsome black boy?'

'You were presentable. A pleasure to look at. You could easily have been my son – I'm presentable, like you. To the average passer-by you would look like my son.'

'By a good-looking black chap. Oh, I'm sure we had people wondering and guessing. You liked being seen with me. For a while that was all I saw in our relationship. Then I realized.'

'Realized what?'

'That I was your revenge. You'd caught up with what was going on between Harry and Cornelia.'

'Nothing was going on.' Claudia's face had become a brilliant red.

'There certainly was. And it continued going on even when she had left this house. She was trapped. She was in a sexual dungeon – trapped into giving Harry what he wanted just so long as he continued to want it.'

'You're talking nonsense. I gave Harry his marching orders a few weeks after she'd gone independent.'

'Yes, you did. You thought giving him the push would end the whole business, but he hung around the band and was introduced to people as its business manager. I used to talk to him now and then, but we never talked about anything of importance. Not him and Corny, nor me and you.'

'No reason why you shouldn't. Corny and you were both of age by then.'

'Then Harry disappeared. I think he got the message that he was trapped in a relationship that was going nowhere. I got the message too. I was being used by you, to get at Harry.'

Claudia nodded vigorously. 'There was real feeling, though – that too. We went together so well, so totally. Your body responded to mine, just as mine responded to you.'

'It didn't.'

'Oh, but it did. Do you think I didn't know about those things? I knew everything about sex, and you were a wonderful learner.'

'No!'

'Yes. You were a joy to be with. I was *proud* to be with you, and proud of things that other people could only guess about.'

'I was just an instrument of revenge. It was payback time. All those times – all those nights. Then I felt I was learning about love. I wasn't. I was being used, and what I was learning about was the art of settling accounts.'

'You should be grateful I taught you so well.'

'Grateful! I feel like I've been smeared from head to foot with shit – the colour of *your* mind, your monstrous ego.'

'I'll say something for the new you: your vocabulary has improved.'

He looked at her with his mouth open. 'Is that all you can say? Was I your one-man Scrabble kit?'

'Not much else. It's not often a sixteen-year-old kid can teach a thirty-two-year-old divorcee much about life and habits, is it?'

He still looked shaken, stunned.

'So you're a divorcee, are you? Luckily I don't need even to go through that tomfoolery. I can just say "it's over" and there's nothing left of you and me.' He ran to the door to the street. 'Goodbye, for good this time. I hope I never see you again – not even to pass you in the street.'

He dashed through it, and slammed it after him.

'Remember my little room, Graham?' said Claudia, pulling the door open again. 'The naughty room? It's still there.'

In the gloom of the hallway she could see the young man's face turned back to her, full of terror.

'I tried to make that as comfortable as could be, you know me – I would, wouldn't I? They had to be punished if they disobeyed the rules, but I made it as easy as I could. None of you really liked it though, did you? I remember you when I finally let you out. It was why you ran away, wasn't it? I have friends, you know, people I can trust. Be careful, Graham. If you're not very careful you might find yourself back there.

Big boy, little room. Not really a room, is it? More like a cage.'

As he turned and made a dash through the door and out into the open street, Claudia's laugh almost become a cackle, following him as his footsteps faded into nothing.

Claudia went into the kitchen. She boiled the kettle and made a pot of tea all to herself. She poured a cup, then helped herself to a biscuit, eating it thoughtfully, with a little smile playing around her lips. Then she put cups and plates under the tap. Then, as an afterthought, she put one of the cups back on the draining board and poured herself yet one more cup of tea. She went out into the hall, then began up the stairs, holding her cup carefully. At the landing she opened a creaky door and began up to the second floor, switching on a dim light as she went. The walls around her sloped alarmingly as the stairs came to another door, and she opened it. She put the cup on an old wooden stool, and looked about her in the light from the doubly-dim twenty-five-watt environmentally friendly bulb.

The cage, which she had tried to make so cosy, was about four feet high, and about the same length square. The only furniture was an old wooden chair which probably went with the table outside – nursery furniture. The man inside, moaning plaintive whines, was dressed only in a heavy overcoat. His face could hardly be seen behind the barrier of moustache and beard – the latter roughly cut away around the chest area. He was making little plaintive sounds, like a distressed puppy or kitten and he cupped his hands towards Claudia, who knew from long habit what the feeble attempts at words were trying to say.

'Mew. Mew.' He tried to put consonants in. 'Mew, Claudia please. Mew.'

'Stop that mewing. It sounds like begging. And you know I never respond.'

The mewing sound got louder.

'Oh no, Harry. You know better than that. You don't get tea till your will has been broken.'

'It is! Mew. It is!'

'Oh, but that's not something you can decide. I do that. You always insisted upon that with the children. Never let out until their wills had been utterly broken. You decided that as I decide it now. Never let out until their wills were utterly smashed. I'd come back from work and find them released, crying, sullen, but totally obedient. It was only slowly that I realized what had gone on. You were betraying me, Harry.'

'Tea, Claudia. Mew. Mew. Tea. Tea.'

'Oh no, Harry. Water. Bread and water. Until you die or I die. Race you there! If I go first you will go very slowly and unpleasantly. You must hope and pray you go first. I would.'

The attempts at words reverted to being little more than whines and mews, even more desperate, and the man – the once man – clung to the bars of his cage, and Claudia saw on his right hand the shape of an engagement ring. It always annoyed her.

'Why Harry, you're more bent than ever! Almost bent double. What a shame! The young girls never fancy a man who's bent crooked. I know I don't. I don't think you'd be successful in breaking their wills now.

'Now, I think I must be going. Lots of things to do – you've no idea. But first . . .'

She delicately took the cup in her hand and tipped its contents on to the bare floorboards. A pathetic mew had risen from the cage.

'What a pity, Harry! If you weren't locked in you could come out and lap up the tea. Like a dog, Harry. Well, I must be going. I'll switch off your light. You must get your beauty sleep, mustn't you?'

And she turned and locked the door to the attic, then began down the rickety stairs. She was unusually happy and began singing. Then she realized her song sounded like Harry's whining and the only word identifiable was 'mew'. She quickly shifted to an early Beatles number.

When she reached the ground floor she looked at the door Graham had come through. 'Tut-tut,' she said, and went and pulled the two bolts over. 'Not much use your keys now, Graham,' she said. She began singing again. The song was very like a repetitive mew again, but she was unaware of that.

In the middle of the hall she stopped, looked around her, and slowly a smile spread over her face. 'A prison,' she said. 'I've made a prison, and a damned good one. And she went along the hall to the kitchen, continuing to sing her prison song.

HECTOR'S OTHER WOMAN
Ann Cleeves

Ann Cleeves has created no fewer than four series of mysteries. Her early books featuring the birdwatching couple George and Molly Palmer-Jones were followed by novels about Inspector Stephen Ramsay, and then by the creation of Vera Stanhope, who has now been brought to the small screen in a series starring Brenda Blethyn. The first book of her Shetland Quartet, *Raven Black*, won the CWA Gold Dagger, and introduced Jimmy Perez.

On impulse Vera took herself off to Holy Island. She had a sudden craving for crab sandwiches and a blast of sea air. Of course she hadn't stopped to check tide times, but arrived at Beal just in time. Hector's Land Rover made it across the causeway as the water was blowing in and the last tourist cars splashed back to the mainland. It was a big tide of the autumn equinox and a blustery north-easterly wind carried sharp showers of rain. Arriving at the Snook there was a rainbow, and Lindisfarne castle in the distance like an illustration from a child's picture book.

The hotel looking over the harbour had rooms free and again on impulse Vera chose the grandest. It was a little shabby but large with windows on two sides, one facing the priory and the other the Herring Houses and the castle beyond. The receptionist made no comment. The island was used to visitors of all sorts: trippers and romantics and pilgrims. Perhaps she thought Vera was a nun in mufti, a nun with expensive tastes.

Vera left her bag in her room and walked out. She hated the island when it was full of visitors, but midweek in November once the tide came in, there were only locals and the occasional mad tourist. Walking through the village she saw there was a house for sale right next to the pub. Perhaps she should retire here once they forced her out of the police service. But she knew she'd never leave the house in the hills, the house where she'd grown up, where she'd lived with Hector. Her father, deceased. The man who most haunted her dreams.

She strode briskly down the straight lonnen, north towards the sea. In the distance there was a lone birdwatcher at the end of the track. He must have disappeared into the dunes because when she looked up again he'd gone. She was heading for the triangular stone that marked Emmanuel Head, for no reason other than that it gave her somewhere to aim for. She wasn't in the mood for wandering without purpose. She lost sight of it occasionally as she followed random paths through the sandy land, but then she emerged at the top of a dune and she was almost on it and there was a view along the beaches on either side of it. Gannets were diving not far from shore and a group of scoter bounced in the choppy water. There was nothing to break the wind here and she found it hard to breathe.

She leaned against the marker stone, sheltering as best she could. Looking back at the island the light was beginning to fade. It wouldn't be dark for a couple of hours, but the colour was seeping out of the grass and the stone.

Then, suddenly, she was pitched back more than thirty years. Another autumn afternoon. Another wild dash to Holy Island just before the tide. Then Hector had been driving and she'd been an unwilling passenger, bullied to accompany him. She'd been in the middle of her A-level year and had been reluctant to leave her books.

'Come on, Vee,' he'd said. 'All work and no play . . .' And she'd done as he'd wanted. Then she always did.

He'd bought her lunch in the Lindisfarne Hotel and drunk too much. Red wine with his steak and whisky after. He talked a lot, became excitable, almost manic. If it had been the spring, Vera would have suspected he was planning a raid on birds' eggs. Hector had been an egg collector all his life; it wasn't a passing childhood phase, but an obsession, a strange passion. It was also a business because he traded the eggs, and collected rare ones on commission. That and a small inheritance from his family was all the family had to live on. The business was illegal of course, and that was why Hector enjoyed it so much: he loved the risk, the possibility that he might be caught.

But that time thirty years ago, it had been autumn too and long past the breeding season. There would be no eggs on the shore or along the edges of the pools. Nothing to steal.

When the time came to pay the bill, Hector pulled his wallet from his jacket pocket. He held it under the table to take out the money, but Vera saw him. She'd always been curious, a child who pried into other people's business. It was stuffed with notes, more cash than she could count. Presumably he'd recently made a good sale. Once he'd sold a young peregrine to an Arab prince and they'd lived well for months.

After lunch Hector said he was going for a walk. 'No need for you to come, Vee.' His tone breezy. 'You can sit in the Land Rover and do some work.' Because that time there had been no hotel room. They planned to leave as soon as the tide ebbed. She waited in the car park until he'd disappeared down the straight lonnen towards the coast. Then she went after him. Partly because she was bored and partly because she didn't trust him. Occasionally he stopped and looked behind him, checking that nobody was following. He hadn't seen Vera. Even then she was a big young woman, but she could move quickly and she knew how to hide, how to fade into the landscape. Hector had taught her well when he'd taken her on his raids in the hills for eggs and young birds of prey.

At Emmanuel Head he'd stopped and looked around him again, this time with more purpose, as if he had an appointment. He even looked at his watch. After a few moments, Vera saw the woman walking along the beach, scattering the wading birds that settled again behind her. It was as if she were kicking up large flakes of confetti. She had red hair and wore wellingtons and a long Barbour coat. Rather county, Vera thought, watching from a distance, but as the woman approached she changed her mind. This woman was pretty not middle-aged horsey, and under the waxed coat she wore a long floral dress. It was the time of Laura Ashley, of high waists and frills. The hair was wild. She could have been an art student and that made her exotic to Vera. She was young, older than Vera but not by more than five or six years. What could her father have to do with this woman?

The couple stood for a moment, looking at each other.

Hector rested his elbow on the back of the wooden bench that stood next to the monument, a way of steadying himself against the wind. Perhaps he was still a little drunk. They didn't touch but they'd met before, Vera was sure of that. Words were exchanged but she was too far away to hear. She tried to read the relationship from the way they were standing, but failed to make sense of it, couldn't decide if it were affectionate or hostile. Now, she thought, she'd make a better fist of it. Now she was more experienced at picking up a gesture, an expression. Then she was young and naïve.

When Hector held up a hand after several minutes of conversation, Vera couldn't tell if he were cautioning patience or asking the woman to wait for him. Or perhaps it was just a stilted way of saying goodbye. In any event he turned away from her and began to walk along the path skirting the shore that led back towards the castle. The woman did wait, her coat pulled around her. As she watched him walk away, she seemed suddenly to shrink. Her shoulders dropped and it was as if the life had been sucked out of her. There was a sense of terrible resignation. Then she straightened her back again and returned to the beach, retracing her own footsteps in the sand.

Vera scrambled up to the triangular marker stone of Emmanuel Head and watched them, far apart on different tracks, making their way down the island. But although they walked separately she had the sense that they were aware of each other's position. This was like a dance with the whole of Holy Island as the ballroom floor. It seemed inevitable that eventually they would come together once more.

Vera decided that she would follow Hector. If she dropped down on to the beach the redhead would notice her. It would be impossible to be quiet with the waders calling whenever they were disturbed. She watched until Hector turned into the crooked lonnen and was hidden by the hedge and then she went after him, moving very quickly, light despite her size. She was close enough to see him turn into the small cottage, hardly more than a shack, which stood surrounded by an overgrown garden. It had a corrugated iron roof, covered in rust, and a small wooden veranda. There were no other houses in this part of the island and now that the light was fading nobody else was about. Hector took a key out of his pocket and let himself in.

The red-headed woman wasn't as quiet as Vera and it was easy to hear her coming down the lonnen. Vera slipped behind a dry stone wall and waited. The woman walked up to the path to the cottage and tapped lightly on the door. Now there was a light inside. Not electric. It flickered. Perhaps the place was so isolated that it had no electricity. A tilley lamp perhaps or calor gas. Hector opened the door and the woman went inside.

'You've decided then?' Hector's voice. Triumphant. A tone Vera knew well. She didn't hear the woman's answer. Or perhaps his companion knew better than to speak when he was in this mood. But how well did she know him? The door was shut. Vera glimpsed him briefly through the window closing the curtains.

She climbed from her hiding place and back to the track. It was almost dark and there were no street lights here. She didn't want Hector to bump into her as she stumbled back to the Land Rover. After all she didn't know how long he would be. How could she explain that she'd been following him?

She didn't take the direct route to the car park. Instead she made her way towards the village. She could always tell Hector that she'd got bored waiting and wandered out in search of a café for tea. Her head was spinning with questions and remembering the woman, standing at Emmanuel Head, the collapse in will and posture as Hector had walked away from her, Vera felt the stirring of anger and defiance. Until then she'd blamed herself for Hector's attitude to her: if she were prettier, thinner, more compliant, he would be different towards her. But the red-headed woman had been pretty and thin and still, it seemed, he felt the need to bully.

Vera didn't want to picture what might be happening in the cottage with the rusting iron roof. Instead she focused on detail. How had Hector got the key? Did the place belong to one of his shady friends: the bizarre and eccentric brotherhood of illicit falconers and taxidermists to which he belonged? Had he stolen it? Blagged it? Hector could lie for

Northumberland and he had no shame. And how had he met the bonny redhead? What could she possibly see in him?

The pub in the main street was already open and Vera stood for a moment looking in through the window. Inside there was a fire and a game was being played. A strange game involving a quoit strung from a rope attached to the ceiling. The players swung the quoit towards a pair of horns fixed to the wall and attempted to loop it on to one of them. An islander pushed his way in from the street and through the briefly opened door Vera heard laughter, smelled beer and the smoke from the driftwood fire. She would have loved to go in but in the Holy Island of the 1970s she knew she wouldn't be welcome. The pub wasn't the place for a young woman to enter alone. Not a stranger. She wandered back to the Land Rover.

Hector arrived just in time for them to follow the tide back to the mainland. In fact he hadn't been in the cottage for more than half an hour. Vera's understanding of sex was rather sketchy. How long did it take to make love? Because she assumed that was what had happened there. Hector hadn't had a regular girlfriend since Vera's mother had died, but somehow he had persuaded the pretty young woman to have sex with him. The redhead hadn't wanted to – that was clear from her attitude at the marker on Emmanuel Head. So he must have had some hold over her. On the journey back to the house in the hills, Hector still seemed elated and excitable. Vera said very little, but no response was expected from her. She wondered what had happened to the sad young woman. Had she stayed on the island or was she driving back to the mainland too?

Thirty-five years later, leaning against the marker stone and feeling the gusts of wind eddy around her, Vera thought that her decision to become a police officer had stemmed from that day. It was the last thing Hector would have wanted for her and that was enough. The next day she'd phoned her local police station and arranged an informal interview. She'd sat her exams and then she'd joined up.

She'd met Hector's redhead, the only other woman in his life it seemed, a few years after she joined the force. There'd been a joint operation and the serious crime squad had come

up from Newcastle. It was the early eighties, a time of big
hair and big shoulder pads, a style that, like the Laura Ashley
ruffles, had passed Vera by. The operation involved local
council corruption, organized crime and an agency supplying
high-class prostitutes. Vera had been seconded to the team,
presumably because there were so few women in the squad.
The meeting had been held in the station in Kimmerston, and
there'd been a pinboard with photos of the main players. Most
of her colleagues smoked and she'd viewed the images through
a haze of cigarette smoke. That was when she'd seen the
woman. Not on the board, staring out at her, but sitting at a
table at the front of the room in conversation with the DCI in
charge of the operation. The wild red hair had been cut and
she wore grey trousers and a black jacket, a neat white blouse.
She looked more like a businesswoman now than a student.

'Who's that?' Vera nodded towards the woman and directed
her question to Sammy Kerr, her sergeant.

'Ah,' he said. 'The lovely Judy Laidlaw. Already a DI.
Ambitious. She's tipped to be the first female chief constable
in the UK. And I wouldn't bet against her.' He paused. 'I'll
introduce you later. She's a great one for getting women into
the CID and I know you'll not be happy until it happens for
you.'

Throughout the meeting Vera watched Laidlaw. The images
she'd constructed around the woman and Hector shifted, as
the patterns in a kaleidoscope change when the tube is turned.
This was a strong woman, with a career of her own. Laidlaw
would be the equal partner in a relationship. What could she
have seen in Hector? Had Vera been wrong? Could they have
cared for each other? Had he met her on other occasions? Or
was something altogether different going on?

When the operation was over – completed successfully in
that the girls and the thugs at the bottom of the heap were
arrested and the politicians and the money men remained
untouched – they all went to a pub in the city centre. Vera
was treated as one of the lads by the men in the team. She
drank pints and didn't ask for favours. Judy Laidlaw was rather
different. She flirted with them, stroking their egos, and they
were queuing up to buy her vodka tonics.

Sammy Kerr was as good as his word and introduced the women. His voice was mellow with beer. 'Meet our Vera,' he said. 'Sharp as a tack. You could use her on your team.' And he melted away towards the bar. In the crowded pub the women could have been alone. They took a small table in a corner and the noise continued away from them.

'Vera?' Laidlaw's eyes were unfocused – the vodka tonics were taking their toll – but her voice was gracious. Still she knew she had it in her power to deliver favours.

'Aye. Vera Stanhope.' Emphasizing the rural accent. She looked up at the inspector. 'I think you know my dad.'

Laidlaw set down her drink. She looked around her to check that her colleagues were out of earshot, and again Vera recognized the despair she'd seen in the woman at Emmanuel Head. 'What do you want?'

'To know what was going on between you and my father.'

'Nothing. Nothing was going on.' A look of distaste. 'Nothing like that.'

'I saw you on Holy Island, one November afternoon.'

Laidlaw gave a tight little laugh. 'He said he'd brought his daughter. Cover, he said, though who would be interested in us?' Then, quite serious: 'You do realize this could ruin me?'

'I want to know.'

Perhaps the drink made Laidlaw reckless, persuaded her that really Vera posed no threat. Or perhaps now she found the secret unbearable. In any event she started talking and the words spilled out. 'I was Northumbria's first Wildlife Liaison Officer. A new post and nobody wanted it. But I knew it would get me noticed and a woman in the force needs all the visibility she can get. You'll understand that.'

Vera nodded.

'Your father did his homework. Checked me out. I was the enemy, the new opposition. I'd head up any investigation into wildlife crime. He discovered that I had a baby and no husband, that I was ambitious. That I was in debt.'

Vera said nothing, but she knew what was coming next. She remembered the wallet packed with cash as Hector paid for the lunch in the Lindisfarne Hotel.

'He offered me money,' Laidlaw said. 'More money than

I'd seen before. I went to the island determined to stand firm. But he persuaded me.'

'Oh yes,' Vera said. 'He can be very persuasive.'

'So after that I turned a blind eye.' The woman shrugged. 'Birds' eggs. That's not real crime, is it?'

'It's against the law,' Vera said, though hadn't she turned a blind eye too? She'd moved out of the house in the hills as soon as she could, but she knew what Hector was up to.

'What will you do?' Laidlaw asked.

'Nothing,' Vera said. 'None of my business.'

And a fortnight later she'd received an application form for a new post in CID.

Now she sat in the bar of the hotel on Holy Island, drinking whisky and re-reading the piece in *The Journal* that had brought her here. An article about recently retired Chief Constable Judith Laidlaw, who had ended her career in Thames Valley, but had begun her service in Northumbria. It seemed she'd already been awarded an OBE in the honours list for her probity and for the quality of her leadership.

Vera went back to the bar and raised a glass to her benefactor, to Hector's other woman.

THE GOLDEN HOUR
Bernie Crosthwaite

Bernie Crosthwaite has had a varied career, including spells as a journalist, tour guide and teacher. She has written plays for radio and theatre and had a number of her short stories broadcast, as well as writing crime novels.

17 August, 20.05 hours

The domestic is a real downer. Wife attacks husband with a cricket bat. Apparently it's been going on for years. It started with punching him, then pulling his hair out in handfuls, then stubbing cigarettes on his bare back. While he's telling us all this the guy is sitting on the floor, whimpering like a dog. That really gets to me.

'What a loser,' says PC Lowery on the way back to the station.

I don't say anything, just take one hand off the wheel and release a strand of hair that's got trapped in my plait. I glance out of the window. After a wet day it's turned into a beautiful evening. The sun is streaking out from under the clouds like fingers. I feel sorry for the kids on their school holidays. It's been a lousy summer.

The duty officer is talking on the phone as we come in. He puts a hand over the mouthpiece. 'Helen – you can take this one. A misper. Caller's name – Mrs Sally Hunter. Try and get some sense out of her.'

He hands me the phone. Brett Lowery pushes past me on the way to the canteen.

'Hello. Mrs Hunter? My name's Sergeant Brandling. What seems to be the—'

'My little – girl – my little – girl . . .' There's a catch in the woman's voice like hiccups.

'Hold on, Mrs Hunter.' I signal for a notepad and pen. 'Tell me exactly what's worrying you.'

'She was playing outside – she's – not there – I don't know – I don't know where . . .' The words are being pulled out of her by force. 'She's . . . disappeared.'

I can barely hear the last word. It's whispered like it's an obscenity.

'Is there anywhere she might have gone?'

'She knows not to leave the garden.'

'Did you check up and down the street?'

'She's as good as gold.'

'Have you looked for her indoors, Mrs Hunter?' It's surprising how many don't, how quickly panic sets in. They're on to the police before they've even searched the house.

'I called her. She always comes when I call.' Her voice is getting higher, close to hysteria.

Obsessive mother, rebellious child? Maybe. But my gut twists. I have a feeling about this one.

'OK, Mrs Hunter. I need a few details. What's your address?' All I get is a weird noise like a howl. 'Try and keep calm, for your little girl's sake.'

She takes a deep breath. 'Thirty-seven, Gunnerston Road.'

'And your daughter's name?'

'Natalie.'

'How old is she?'

'Eight and a half.'

'Can you tell me what clothes she's wearing?'

'A pink and white sundress and pink sandals.'

'And what does she look like?'

'She's quite small for her age. Light brown hair. Green eyes.' Her voice falls away as if she'll never see those green eyes again.

'OK. I'll get her description circulated straight away and I'll be with you in about ten minutes. Please listen carefully, Mrs Hunter. As soon as you put the phone down I want you to have a good look round the house, and check the garden and any outbuildings or sheds. Will you do that, please?'

'But she isn't—'

'The most likely thing is that Natalie's hiding. Let's hope

you find her before we get there. That'll be the best outcome for everyone.'

As soon as the call ends I give the duty officer my notes and he starts logging them into the system. 'And can you check the database for known paedophiles in the Gunnerston Road area?'

I'm up the stairs two at a time. Brett's in the canteen, just about to stuff a bacon sandwich down his neck.

'Forget that. You're coming with me.'

I give Brett the few details I have as we clatter down the stairs. The duty officer looks up from his computer and shakes his head.

No leads then. Nothing to point us in the right direction. We'll have to start from square one.

As we run towards our patrol car I check the time. Quarter past eight. If we can find Natalie Hunter within the hour the odds are she'll still be alive. As time passes the odds worsen. A day without a sighting and it's fifty-fifty. After that we could be looking at a murder investigation. The next sixty minutes are crucial.

The golden hour starts now.

I've been waiting for an evening like this for a long time.

I had planned to take the Norton to the coast today. I got all my equipment ready last night. But when I woke up this morning it was wet and the rain was forecast to last for hours. It was almost certain there would be a sea fret, a 'haar' as they call it in Scotland, and the thought of riding all that way in the rain to find nothing but thick white fog was unappealing and I abandoned the trip.

It's been a frustrating day, spent staring out of the window and reading my monthly photography magazine. I read the many articles on digital techniques with deep misgivings. I'm not against the new technology. I recently invested in a very expensive digital camera and I've played around with images, but it feels like a form of cheating. Capturing my subject in all its perfection has always been the challenge for me.

With dinner eaten, the dishes washed up and put away and nothing on television but wall-to-wall rubbish I'm lost for something to do. Since I retired, if I can't get out with my camera, time hangs heavy.

When I take the bin bag out I see that the sky is no longer a uniform grey pall. The clouds are beginning to break up and rays of sunshine, like the spokes of a fan, shoot out and touch the ground with gold. The correct name for them is crepuscular rays. Some people call them the fingers of God.

My camera bag is already packed. The motorbike has a sidecar, which Lynette never liked, but she isn't here any more and that means there's more room for bulkier equipment like the tripod. I'm ready to go within minutes. And all the time, the sky is changing, the clouds dissolving and reforming in unpredictable patterns.

I feel my excitement rise. Along with dawn, around sunset is one of the best times of day to take pictures.

We call it the golden hour.

20.19 hours

Gunnerston Road is a steep street with houses built against the slope. The garden of number 37 is terraced to cope with the gradient – concrete beds filled with bushy heathers. There's a steep winding flight of steps up to the front door. We're both breathing hard by the time we get there.

The door is opened by a small plump woman around forty.

'Mrs Hunter? Sergeant Helen Brandling. And this is PC Lowery.'

She doesn't look us in the eye. She seems mesmerized by our uniforms. Then her gaze darts behind us, up and down the street.

'Can we come in?'

She steps back. A grandfather clock takes up a lot of space in the narrow hallway and we have to shuffle past it to close the door.

'Any sign of Natalie?'

'No. I've searched the house. I can't find her anywhere.'

'I want you to call her friends. She may have gone off to play with someone without telling you.'

'She'd never do that.'

'It's worth a try.' I look at Brett and nod. He starts to climb the stairs.

'Where's he going? I told you – I've looked all over!'

'No harm in double-checking.'

I've known kids hide in the tiniest spaces – the drawer under the bed, behind the bath, the gap between the wardrobe and wall. Sometimes they're not hiding at all – they've been hidden. What's left of them.

'Is your husband at home?'

Her eyes flicker nervously, looking everywhere but me. 'No.'

'Working late?'

'He left us. About six months ago.'

'I'm sorry.' I wait no more than a heartbeat before I ask, 'Have you got a recent photo of him?'

She leads me into a small cramped living room and points to the mantelpiece. 'I keep it for Natalie's sake.'

A pudgy face, florid complexion, receding hair, rimless glasses.

'Is he fond of Natalie? Does he miss her?'

'Of course.' She looks at me directly for the first time. 'You think Gareth might have . . .?'

'What's his current address?'

She finds it for me. I write it down and ask her what car he drives and the registration. Then I point to the phone in the hall. 'Try everyone you can think of – friends, relatives, neighbours, anyone Natalie might have gone off with. But don't ring your husband, OK?'

I hurry down the hall to the kitchen, a gloomy sunless room with units made of dark wood. I open the back door. It's warmer outside than in the cheerless kitchen. I phone HQ and give them Gareth Hunter's description, address and details of his car, a silver Honda Civic.

The back garden slopes upward to a high fence. It has a crowded neglected feel. A search in the thick shrubs reveals a rubber ball, the arm of a doll and a pink scrunchie, muddy and sodden as if it's been there a long time.

The door of the rickety shed gapes open. There are empty plant pots, old bikes, a rusty pushchair. I shift the heavy bags of compost. An enormous spider runs out and scuttles across the wooden floor. There are no locked cupboards or old fridges, no hidden trapdoors.

I walk through the kitchen as Brett comes down the stairs. Mrs Hunter puts the phone down. We stare at each other blankly. Natalie's mother is the first to look away.

'PC Lowery and I are going to start knocking on doors up and down the street.'

The grandfather clock strikes the half hour. Fifteen minutes into the enquiry already and we have nothing.

'Don't give up, Mrs Hunter. Somebody must have seen her.'

They call it a lake but in reality it's a flooded gravel pit. It has a slightly bleak artificial look about it – too symmetrical perhaps and the steep sides are banks of pebbles rather than vegetation. But it has a certain wild appeal and over the years it's become a beauty spot, a bird sanctuary, even the sailing club uses it.

I drive along the rough path beside the water. Motor vehicles are not strictly allowed but I'm in a hurry and take the chance that at this hour the place will be deserted. The rain-washed sky is filled with furiously active cloud formations which I long to capture, not to mention the shot I've come here for – the water gleaming like satin and boiling clouds backlit by the setting sun.

I don't see anyone, but just in case, I park the bike off the track in a copse of trees. I can't wait to get started. I'm not a professional photographer. I'm not interested in profit. The paps are always looking for the 'money shot' – a drunken politician or a celebrity half naked on a beach. It doesn't seem to matter how blurred or badly composed the picture is, they can still make a small fortune from it. But that's not my way. I only want perfection. With me it's a labour of love.

20.37 hours

I'm doing the evens, Brett Lowery the odds. Climbing up and down the steep steps to each house is exhausting and time-consuming. This is only the third house I've tried. Number 24.

Male, twenties, wearing a loose T-shirt and baggy shorts.

His legs are deeply tanned and muscular, tattoos on each arm, shaven head. He smells clean and soapy as if he's just had a shower. There's a dog too, an Alsatian. The man hangs on to its collar even though it looks old and tired. A retired police dog perhaps. I don't ask. There isn't time.

While I introduce myself and get his name he looks shifty. 'What's this about?'

'A missing person enquiry. Just a routine house-to-house, Mr Corby. Nothing to worry about.'

He relaxes slightly and I ask him if he's seen anything unusual in the neighbourhood today.

'What time?'

'This evening, around seven or eight o'clock?'

'I went to the off-licence at half seven.' A yeasty gust of beer from his belly confirms this.

'Did you see any children playing?'

'Yeah, suppose. But I couldn't tell you which ones. I don't take any notice of kids.'

'OK. Thanks, Mr Corby.' I flip my notebook shut.

'Hold on.' He scratches his neck with his free hand. 'There was a car driving dead slow. Old guy on a motorbike nearly went into the back of it. I saw it on the way to the offy and again on the way home. It was going the other way then, like it was lost or something, looking for a house number. They're hard to see cos of the steps'

'A silver Honda?' I shouldn't have said that, put words in his mouth.

'No. It was red. A Vauxhall. It was making a chugging noise, like there was a hole in the exhaust or something. Maybe that's why I clocked it.'

'Any chance you noticed the car registration?'

'Nah.' Mr Corby lets go of the dog and it flops down with exhaustion, its tongue lolling sideways. 'Apart from the letters.'

I open my notebook. 'What were they?'

'E-T-C. Et cetera. Geddit? That tickled me, don't know why.' His grin reveals even white teeth, apart from one missing canine, lower right.

'How many people were in the car?'

'Just the bloke driving.'

'Can you describe him?'

'Just a bloke, nothing special about him as far as I can remember.'

'OK, Mr Corby.'

He comes down the top few steps to see me off the premises. That's when he notices the police car, parked outside the Hunters' house.

'It's not little Natalie, is it? Has she gone missing? Has some bastard taken her?'

I fetch the tripod from the sidecar and begin to set it up. The sky is dissolving from blue-gold to mauve. As I hastily release the telescopic legs of the tripod I catch the skin of my finger and reel back with the intensity of the pain, only eased by sucking on the wound. The skin is inflamed but not ruptured, which is a great relief. I once ruined a shot of snowy mountains with a bloody fingerprint on the lens.

I attach the camera to the tripod. I've decided on my new digital model, a Canon that is capable of shooting eight frames a second and has an inbuilt spirit level to make sure the horizon is straight. Then I begin to compose the shot. I fiddle with the equipment until I have the exact angle I want. A sudden ray of bright sun from behind a cloud causes a burst of flare, which is normally regarded as a fault. But it can create unexpectedly interesting effects so I take the shot anyway.

The sky is tinged with pink now. It's becoming more dramatic every second. I take a few more shots but I'm simply flexing my muscles for the big one, the image that will combine the elements of sky, cloud, water and the blood-red light of the final moments of sunset. I suppose it's a bit like capturing the last breath of someone dying.

20.41 hours

My phone rings as I reach the bottom of the steps of number 24. They've traced Natalie's father. He's been fifty miles away all day on business. No sign of a little girl in his rented flat or in his car.

'Shit.'

Brett Lowery runs across the road towards me.

'Have they found her?'

'No such luck.'

He swivels away from me, a grim look on his face.

'Anything from the door-to-door?'

'Nothing. You?'

'Not much. A cruising car, half a registration.'

'It's worth a try, isn't it?'

'Why not? We've got bugger all else.'

Redness is staining the sky, most intense near the horizon, then becoming paler, like ink in water. My finger rests lightly on the shutter.

Then I hear something, a faint rattling noise that disturbs the tranquillity of the lake. It sounds like a car whose engine isn't tuned properly. It's getting louder. I look up from the viewfinder. After a few seconds I see it, a red car bumping along the same track I used earlier. I shrink back into the gloom of the trees. The car drives past but to my horror it stops a little way along the track, just where I have angled the camera towards the lake to capture the finest view.

I'm almost ready to shoot and there is a bright red car slap bang in the middle of my carefully composed shot.

20.49 hours

We carry on knocking on doors, all the while on tenterhooks, waiting for information on the Vauxhall. An old man keeps me talking. He doesn't know anything, he's just glad of the excitement. A couple of others resent being taken away from the footie on telly and can't wait to shut the door in my face. No one except Mr Corby saw a red car cruising up and down the street around half past seven.

My phone rings.

'I've got a trace on a red Vauxhall Astra, G92 ETC, probably stolen as the car is registered to a spinster lady of seventy-five.'

'Last seen when?'

'CCTV on Victoria Road at . . . 20.10. Again at the Mill Lane roundabout at 20.14.'

'Could you see which exit he took?'

'Going towards Steelbridge. We lose sight of him after that – he doesn't appear on the retail park camera a mile down the road.'

I wave frantically at Brett Lowery across the street and he comes running. We jump into the car at the same moment and I drive off with a screech of tyres.

'There's a map on the back seat. Find the Mill Lane roundabout.'

Brett studies the map then jabs it with his finger. 'Got it.'

'Take the Steelbridge exit. Now tell me what's off that road before you get to the shopping mall.'

He traces the route. 'There's a big housing estate. He could be taking her to where he lives.'

My heart sinks. If he's garaged the car then it's going to be a needle and haystack job. 'OK. We'll come back to that possibility. What else?'

'Industrial park. Sixth form college. Further on there's a narrow lane down to a lake but it's not much more than a track.'

'The gravel pit?'

'It says *lake* here.'

'Same thing.'

The roundabout is coming up. I swing on to it, taking the Steelbridge exit. I know the track to the lake. I used to go there years ago with my mates. Lager and ciggies and skimming flat stones on the still flat water.

'What do you think?' asks Brett.

I'm not thinking, not really. I'm relying on instinct, experience, gut feeling. All I know is that time is running out and I've got to make a choice.

It's still there, a bright red blot on the landscape. And all the time the sky is changing, deepening like a developing print, rushing towards the perfect moment.

I'm tempted to go and remonstrate with the driver, but what if he turns nasty? No doubt he's come here to see the sunset too, but I just wish he would move fifty metres along.

There's movement inside the car. Are there two of them? For God's sake. If they're lovers they could be here for ages. And once they start snogging they'll miss the sunset anyway. I stand there helplessly, watching my hopes die.

But the shadow puppets inside the car shift. The door opens, a man wearing a grey tracksuit gets out. He's pulling something. No. Someone. A little girl in a pink and white dress.

Father and daughter then. What are they doing here? The child is dragging her footsteps. It's way past her bedtime. Surely they aren't going for a walk at this time of night, leaving their car stuck in the middle of my shot?

They enter the wood just a few metres away. Now is the moment to confront him and calmly state my case, but he's striding along with a glazed expression that unnerves me and I draw back, crouching down into the undergrowth. Perhaps the little girl just needs a pee, in which case they won't be long. Maybe I can salvage something from this disaster after all.

From my hiding place I watch them approach. The man looks tense, even angry. The child is being pulled along unwillingly. Why is she resisting if she needs to go to the toilet? She seems tired and scared. There's something wrong here but I'm not sure what it is. Saliva rushes into my mouth. I swallow. I have an odd feeling that I should do something, but what?

They pass by so close I can hear his laboured breathing and her moans of distress. They disappear into the wood behind me.

The sky is beautiful – scudding pewter clouds against scarlet, deepening every second. That's my business, that's what I'm here for. The man, the little girl – they have nothing to do with me. I just wish they would go away.

21.04 hours

The track around the lake is rough and bumpy, not meant for motor vehicles. The exhaust bangs on a stray rock.

'Over there.' Brett points across the lake to where a red car is parked next to a clump of trees.

'Get on the Airwave and call for back-up,' I tell him. 'And ask them to put the helicopter on standby.'

We rise inches into the air as I take a curve too sharply. Brett gives me a look but I don't care if I trash the car. I don't care if the driver of the red car hears us coming. I know the track becomes impassable beyond those trees except on foot so he can't escape in that direction. If he drives towards us we'll throw a stinger in his path and wreck his tyres. Personally I would happily crash into him and bring him to a halt that way. But it's not an option. Natalie might be in the car. She's what matters. She's all that matters.

Even before I've come to a standstill Brett is out of the car and running. He yanks open the doors of the Astra then the boot.

'Empty!' he shouts.

I stand between the two cars and scan the scene. The track is deserted up ahead. The water is silky smooth, unruffled. I turn towards the trees. Something glints in the light from the bright red sunset. Metal? Glass? There's movement. A man. Grey hair, beard, leather jacket. He looks startled, steps back and disappears.

Brett's seen him too. He rushes ahead of me into the bushes.

'Get him!' I scream. 'Get the bastard!'

I can't believe it when I hear the second car, coming fast along the track as if this is Silverstone or something. Joyriders, no doubt. I expect to hear loud music coming from the car's speakers, but as I stand up I see with a shock the jazzy blue and yellow flashes. Police.

A young man in uniform leaps out and checks the red car. A female officer joins him. The car is empty. I could have told them that. They look round in desperation.

Sky and water have almost reached the moment of perfection I have been waiting for so patiently. If they find what they're looking for and go away I might yet capture a truly glorious shot.

I take a few steps forward. When they see me, both of them have the same look of disgust and hatred in their eyes. The man hurtles towards me. Some deep blind instinct tells me to turn and run.

I can hear him close behind me, crashing through the bushes. He grabs me round the waist and knocks me to the ground. I feel my right shoulder bone crunch. I lie there winded and shocked.

'Where is she?' he yells. 'What have you done with her?'

Now the woman is towering over me, her face tight. 'Tell us where she is.'

'Who?' My voice is shaking. It sounds weak and pitiful but all my strength has drained out of me.

'The little girl. Natalie. What have you done with her?

I raise my left hand – the right one seems to have lost all connection to my body – and point to the trees. 'In there. Both of them.'

They glance at each other.

'Both?' asks the woman. 'You mean . . . there are two girls?'

'No. A child and a man.'

The male officer sets off but she calls him back.

'You stay with him. I'll go.'

21.07 hours

The bit of daylight that's left barely penetrates in here. I switch on my torch, pointing it down, and inch my way forward. I strain my ears, listening for human sounds beneath the rustle of leaves, the movement of small creatures, the soft breeze that cools the sweat on my back.

I go deeper and deeper into the wood, searching for a ribbon, a strand of brown hair caught on a bush. Anything.

There's a sudden commotion behind me. I swing round and bring the torch level. I see a man running through the under-growth, arms flailing, heading back towards the lake.

'Brett! He's coming your way!'

'We saw something shining,' says the policeman. He swipes at the tree branches.

I struggle up from where I'm squatting on a patch of damp moss. 'It's my camera.'

'Show me.'

I lead him to where the Canon still sits on the tripod.

'Did you take pictures of them?'

'No, of course not. I specialize in landscapes.' I point to the

lake and the spectacular sunset. 'I was all set up and ready when that man, not to mention you and your colleague, came along and ruined my shot.'

'Ruined your shot?' His voice is full of contempt. 'You saw a man take a little girl into the woods and all you cared about was taking snaps?'

'It was none of my business.'

He bunches his fist and draws his arm back. But at the last moment he slaps his arm down by his side. He takes a running kick at the tripod. It keels over and smashes on to the ground.

'Have you any idea how much that camera cost?'

From the look on his face he's going to tell me what I can do with my precious camera. But in the distance we can hear the woman shouting. The man in the tracksuit bursts through the trees. The policeman barges him in the stomach. He collapses, grunting loudly. The officer kneels on him, takes handcuffs from his pocket and secures his wrists behind his back. The man utters an obscenity then lies quiet.

21.13 hours

'Natalie?'

She's lying very still under a tree. Her dress is muddy and torn. She's wearing one pink sandal. The other lies on the ground, exposing a smooth pale foot.

'Natalie,' I whisper. 'It's all right. It's all right now.'

But my throat is thick. It's not all right. It will never be all right.

I gently touch her leg. Still warm. Her arm, her cheek.

Her eyelids flutter.

'Natalie!' I don't mean to shout but I can't help it. She flinches. Her eyes shoot open with terror.

'I'm a police officer,' I say quietly. She puts her arms out to me and my heart buckles. I hold her tight.

The world has gone mad. The air is filled with the sound of sirens. Two more police cars arrive and the man in the track-suit is bundled into the back of one of them.

The female officer emerges from the woods, carrying the

little girl. The child clings to her like a young chimp clings to its mother, arms circling her neck, legs gripping her waist like a vice. She walks past me, without so much as a glance, but when she reaches her colleague I hear her tell him to get my details. She places the child in the back seat of her car and gets in the front.

The young man takes my name and address. 'We'll be in touch,' he says, and spits on the ground. Not a word of apology for the injuries I've suffered or the damage he's done to my equipment.

There's a lot of noise as the cars perform complicated turning manoeuvres on the narrow track. Then they roar off towards the main road.

Peace at last.

I tentatively swing my arm. There's some pain, but it's not, after all, a broken clavicle. I should be able to handle the bike. I pack up the camera and tripod. If the Canon is ruined it will be a great loss. But in some ways the greater loss is my failure to get the picture I crave. These opportunities don't occur very often. I have other cameras but who knows when there will be another evening like this?

Now the clouds have lost all definition and interest. The lake is a dark pool and in the sky, there's just a prosaic red glow. I watch, filled with regret, until the sun goes down.

Night falls.

The golden hour is over.

EXPULSION FROM EDEN
Judith Cutler

Judith Cutler is a prize-winning short story writer and the author of over twenty novels. A former Secretary of the Crime Writers' Association, she lives in Kent with her husband Keith Miles, a fellow crime novelist.

Exeter, 1813

Teigngrace Hall, in the County of Devon, was my favourite of the Earl of Teignbridge's establishments. Very commodious and set in extensive parkland, it lay near the main roads to Newton Abbot and Exeter. It was a veritable paradise, with not even a poacher to spoil the calm air.

My employer, Lord Teignbridge, was a most learned man, eschewing outdoor pleasures, but not denying them to his guests. Indeed, her Ladyship, quite unequal to the rigours of his Lordship's scholarship, whipped in any of either sex who would acquit themselves honourably on the hunting field.

Both hosted the dinner parties, musical evenings and balls for their guests, though that was where their participation ended. It was rightly assumed that I, as butler, and Mrs Lacock, the housekeeper, would see to all the guests' creature comforts.

For luncheon and for dinner, which was eaten at London hours, our honoured French chef, M. Alphonse, actually from the Isle of Man, would send up an elegant repast; my selection from His Grace's cellar always complemented it perfectly.

The only place where guests were not welcome was Lord Teignbridge's library – no ordinary book room. In many other establishments, a room the length of the house would have been the long gallery, the social hub of the house. In Teigngrace, however, a mezzanine floor had been installed over half the width, for the portraits and other masterpieces, great and small. The lower half became the library, the piers which supported the gallery providing bays for all the shelves of weighty tomes.

Lord Teignbridge had made the study of Italian religious paintings his life's work. Occasionally he would permit a scholar – a man from Vienna or Rome, perhaps – to feast his eyes on one masterpiece or another, and they would refer constantly to these works of scholarship.

One, Signor Polpetti, was currently a house guest, having written imploring His Grace to accommodate him at very short notice. Unlike his fellow scholars, Signor Polpetti was a man of the world, flirting shamelessly with many of the younger ladies.

The damsels had plenty of other more eligible suitors, of course: what else is a country house party but a marriage mart in miniature? There were two heirs to titles, including Sir Harry Croyde, who might have lost an arm in Spain, but had thereby gained romantic interest, and a smattering of second sons, including Lord Fowey's youngest lad, who had taken Holy Orders. The Reverend Dr Shaldon – he was a gifted scholar as well as a handsome young man – was unfailingly polite even to the servants, and tireless in standing up to dance with the plainest females. He was perhaps inclined to Methodism, and insisted on leading daily prayers for all the household, family, guests and servants.

At the end of each evening, Mrs Lacock and I would take tea together, while we reviewed the day's work, and the accomplishments or failings of our underlings. Today, however, it was not a servant but a guest who was remiss.

Mrs Lacock leaned forward confidentially. 'I have received a welter of complaints about one of His Grace's guests, who seems to lurk in every corner. My girls are all good, virtuous creatures, and deserve to be treated as such.'

'Signor Polpetti?'

She nodded.

'I thought as much. But he, being a foreigner, may not understand what is expected of him – or rather, what is not expected.'

'I hear he is as free with the young ladies – but at least

they have their mamas to protect them. These innocent country girls have no one. What can we do?'

'It's no use my speaking to His Grace, Mrs Lacock – I sometimes fear he does not understand what a young girl is, unless she is mother naked and in a gilded frame. So a word in Lady Teignbridge's ear, perhaps?'

'Since he doesn't ride, she probably doesn't know him from Adam – except, of course, that he is better dressed.' She permitted herself a smile. 'He is particular in his attentions to two girls, neither more than fourteen. Pretty young Nan, who used to be his chambermaid. Needless to say I have moved her to other duties, out of harm's way. And that new girl, the quiet one. Molly Abbott. I thought, since she was so plain, she might escape his attentions, but it seems I was mistaken.'

'Plain? I had not thought her plain. Serious, maybe,' I mused. 'As if guarding a secret, even.'

'Secret! Let me tell you straight, Mr Dawson, I like to know where those wenches are every hour of every day – and night. I want no harbouring of secrets!'

I dropped a hint to the footmen: if they felt a guest were stealing kisses or more from any of their female colleagues, they should consider it their duty most discreetly to intervene. Just a cough, perhaps, to indicate that the would-be seducer did not go unseen. Perhaps, even, a false message that the maid was wanted elsewhere. The girls' virtue must not go unprotected.

As I had spoken out for her, I felt it incumbent on me to watch out for young Molly Abbott. And I fear I did not like what I saw. Or rather, did not see. For all Mrs Lacock's strict timetable, there were definitely moments when she was not where she ought to be. But next moment, it seemed, there she was, doing exactly what she had been told, and doing it well. In fact, it would be hard to have found a more efficient girl. She would finish her task quietly and swiftly and then, bobbing a polite curtsy, head off for her next, minutes early. But she would arrive minutes late to start it. Once I thought she might be concealing something under her apron, but I might have been mistaken. Certainly I could see nothing missing, or even out of place. I should have reported her to Mrs Lacock, of course. Call me soft-hearted, but I just could not do it. So one morning I resolved to do what I should have done earlier. I would tail her.

Before I could start on this humiliating mission, I was summoned to the library. Never had His Grace sounded his bell with such urgent passion. I found him in the greatest distress. Indeed, he could not speak. Seizing me by the hand, he almost dragged me up the stairs to his gallery.

He pointed.

Against the silk wallcovering, a small, brighter rectangle stood out. A picture was missing! Not only had Adam and Eve been expelled from the garden, they had left the gallery altogether, and not by his choice.

An immediate summons went out to our parish constable, and ere long we heard the peal of the great doorbell resound through the house. However much I wished that Mr Voke should present himself more properly at the tradesmen's entrance, I could not fault him on his punctuality.

I attended him immediately.

Jedediah Voke, summoned from goodness knows what parochial transgression, was red in the face with his exertions. Without waiting for an invitation, he sank on to one of the heavily carved chairs in the hall, staring about him. He removed from his coat pocket a disreputable clay pipe, but, interpreting aright my astonished cough, he put it to his lips unlit. The family portraits gazed down, the Lely eyebrows lifted in surprise that such a low form of life as Jedediah Voke should be seated beneath them.

Indeed, he might have stepped straight from a comedy by the Bard, his red face, sleepy eyes and slow delivery giving the impression that he was naught but a yokel. Therein lay his strength as an investigator. No one suspected how shrewd he might be. If you put him, however, in the old-fashioned powdered wig and well-cut coat of a magistrate, you would be struck by the intelligence of his brow.

'Let me take you to His Grace,' I said quietly.

'All in good time. Tell me all you know, Mr Dawson,' he said, lowering his voice not a jot.

Aware of all the unseen ears, I ushered Mr Voke swiftly behind the green baize door. It is said that while a member of the nobility is born with a silver spoon in his mouth, a good butler is born with a brass padlock to his lips. Silver bends, of course, but never underestimate the strength of a butler's discretion.

Before I could speak, there was a soft tap at the door. Mrs Lacock slipped in. Her underlings as much as my own would be under suspicion.

'Now, tell me all you know – and then Mrs Lacock can do the same. I want to address His Grace with the authority of knowledge,' he declared. 'This picture. What was it of?'

'It was indecent, if you ask me. I didn't like my girls going anywhere near it. Not that His Grace let them. He said it was too precious to endanger with even a feather duster. Did you ever hear the like?'

'So it had people in it in a state of undress?' he suggested, licking a pencil and applying it firmly to his notebook.

'Naked but for well-placed tendrils,' I said, loftily, as befitted a man of the world.

'The subject was . . . biblical,' Mrs Lacock agreed. 'The Fall of Man. Aye, and woman too.'

'I didn't see a gap in the pictures in the hall.'

'It was in the gallery, almost His Grace's private room.'

'Private? A man likes to show off his pictures.'

I nodded. 'Many are the acres of naked limbs I have seen, Mr Voke, struggling with this monster or that, or being chased in battle. Indeed, you may find the like in many of our corridors. But this small item was one of His Grace's favourites. He spoke of it being by a man called Michelangelo.'

'Did he indeed? And who might have been a-looking at it lately?'

'Signor Polpetti,' Mrs Lacock and I said as one.

He pulled a puzzled face, but inscribed the name. 'And anyone else?'

'That you would have to ask His Grace,' I said.

'And what about these here maids, with or without their dusters? Who is responsible for cleaning the room?'

Mrs Lacock said firmly, 'The older, most experienced ones.

But let me see – because this signor cannot keep his hands to himself, I took the girl who normally sees to it and sent her to do his chamber instead. The new girl ended up in the library.'

'And the new girl is?'

'Young Molly Abbott. From Moretonhampstead originally. I thought I could trust her not to have an attack of the vapours every time she saw things she ought not to.'

Voke made another note. 'While I am speaking to His Grace, I would like all the men and maids gathered together so I might speak to them. And find some excuse to keep the ladies and gentleman in. The weather, I should think. 'Tis like to be mortal bad, tell them. And that's no lie, either,' he added, as I raised an eyebrow at the bright sunlight outside. 'You mark my words.'

His Grace had made rare inroads into the brandy decanter.

'The work is priceless,' he said, 'and eminently portable. Though others dispute it, I believe it is Michelangelo's original sketch for the masterpiece now in the Sistine Chapel! *Original Sin*. The expulsion from the Garden of Eden. Everything about it speaks of its quality – it must be, *is*, by the greatest of the Italian masters! And now it is gone! It may be halfway across the Channel by now!'

'And a lot of good it'll do the thief to end up in Old Boney's hands,' Voke said, carefully measuring the bright space left behind. 'But I'll send my best lads to alert the harbour authorities in Newton, Teignmouth and Exeter. Though it'd puzzle a foreigner to find any of them the way the weather's closing in. You won't see your hand before your face within the hour, you mark my words.'

As one we looked out of the window: Devon mist was indeed swirling around, as if someone were waving a giant grey scarf in the air.

'Your Grace, have any of your guests lingered over this picture longer than most?'

'They are guests! They are gentlemen!'

'Even this Italian man?'

'Polpetti? A gentleman and a scholar. An honourable man!'

'Any others?'

'Fowey's lad.'

'That'd be Dr Shaldon,' I explained. But as a Methodist, what would he be doing looking at such papist stuff?

'Anyone else?'

'One of the tweenies – she seemed mighty taken with it. No idea what she's called.'

Of course. They were trained to be invisible. But for all that I could see one face in my mind's eye – that of Molly Abbott. And things were not looking good for her, not at all.

They looked even worse when I saw her gathered with the other staff in the servants' hall. She kept pressing her hands to her little white face, and looking anxiously out of the window.

Jedediah Voke looked sternly about him. I had no doubt he noted Molly's pallor too, and made the same damning assessment as I did. But he said nothing, simply explaining what had happened and asking for help: 'Folk like you aren't supposed to be seen, but I warrant you see more than you let on,' he added.

To my amazement M. Alphonse stepped forward. 'I can tell you one thing for nothing,' he said, his French accent much lighter than usual. 'That Signor Polpetti is no more Italian than I am. Polpetti, indeed. What sort of man goes round calling himself Mr Meatballs? A charlatan, Mr Voke, that's what our Signor Polpetti is.'

Voke jotted swiftly.

No one else stepped forward, so at last, with an adjuration to keep their eyes open and their mouths shut, I sent them about their business.

Molly Abbott hung back – no doubt about it. Voke noticed. 'Many's the guilty party who wants to get the crime off their chest,' he said, in a hoarse whisper. 'Let's talk to her.'

By now she was wringing her hands and pleating her apron. 'Sir, I know I should not put myself forward, but I do fear the moors in this weather.'

Voke frowned. 'And what has that to do with anything?'

'Young Dr Shaldon's out there, sir. He slipped out early, while I was dusting.'

'He must have slipped out from somewhere,' Voke observed. 'And I deduce it would not be through the front door.'

'No indeed, sir. But I dare not say more. I fear for my place here, sir.'

'And why should that be?'

'I cannot tell you, sir. I truly cannot!' With that she burst into tears. 'But I promise you, sir, I was doing no wrong.' She fled.

Mrs Lacock, who had been watching silently from the back of the room, caught my eye. 'Let her have her cry,' she said, 'and then I will speak to her. She will not leave this house, never fear.'

'So the Meatballs man isn't what he seems, and young Dr Shaldon is missing. And a housemaid is in hysterics. Where do we proceed from here?' Mr Voke was nursing a small glass of the estate cider.

'I fear I have been sadly remiss,' I confessed. 'I knew that little Molly was behaving oddly, and have done nothing about it. She slips into rooms late, and out early. But she accomplishes her duties excellently.'

'And do we know where she goes between tasks?'

I shook my head. 'I had it in mind to follow her. But such a thing would be demeaning, would it not?'

Voke gave a lopsided smile. Of course, that was what he did all the time. By way of silent apology, I topped up his glass.

He sipped. 'We have a room not open to everyday guests. We have two scholars permitted to study a priceless picture. And we have a tearful maid, whose duties take her into the vicinity of the picture, worried about the whereabouts of one of the guests. Is he handsome, Mr Dawson? Aye, I feared so. And she is smitten, poor wench. Well, I am tempted to go by her instincts, Mr Dawson – I suspect the young clergyman may be on the Haldon road. And I suspect he is carrying something of interest. Meanwhile, let us speak to Mr Meatballs.'

But by whatever name he went, he was nowhere to be found either.

Whatever Mrs Lacock said to Molly, it only served to make her more tearful. So eventually Mr Voke said, 'Let me talk to the little maid. I do believe I'm acquainted with her uncle by marriage on her father's side. Let us see how that approach may work. Yes, you may listen, Mr Dawson, but I'd rather she didn't know you were there. And I'd rather you kept quieter than a church mouse, whatever she may tell me. Agreed?'

As a butler, I take orders from no one but His Grace. But if I failed to agree, the interview would take place without my knowing anything that passed, so I concurred. To overhear conversations without giving the participants any idea of my presence is not unusual for one in my position. The only difference I anticipated was that at least I would have the chance to discuss this encounter afterwards.

Voke must have talked Moretonhampstead gossip for at least ten minutes before Molly responded – and if I tell you that while the town has a long and venerable past, it is still a very small place, you will understand how tedious those ten minutes were. However, I did learn that young Molly was a favourite of the late parson's wife, and would have liked to continue in her service but that on her husband's death the good widow was forced to go and live with her family. I also learned that one of her tasks had been to read aloud to the lady.

Read! A village girl like that knowing her letters well enough to read aloud! The notion made me gasp. The Bible, poetry and sermons! Whatever next? Novels? I found it hard to keep my promise and my silence.

'So when I can, I try to keep up my reading, Mr Voke. To keep the words in my head, you might say.'

'And where would you be doing this here reading, Miss Molly?'

There was a long pause. 'Once or twice in my bed, but then I think Mr Dawson saw me carrying a book, so I stopped. So now it's in the library, sir. Most often His Grace doesn't even know I'm there. If he does, I flaps my duster and he thinks I'm carrying out my duties.'

'I think you should show me exactly where.'

My heart bled at the depth of her sigh. 'Of course, sir. But please sir, for pity's sake, send after Dr Shaldon. A stranger's like to perish when the fret comes in like this.'

'Lord bless you, Molly – don't you worry about that.'

Nor need she, the head keeper and a team of outdoor servants having been already despatched on Voke's orders.

'Tell me, my girl, are you keeping company with some fine
young lad?'

In the silence, I could almost see her hung head and deep,
painful blush.

'What, no sweetheart? What are the young men thinking
of, not courting the cleverest girl for miles round? And are
you sweet on anyone? Dr Shaldon, maybe?'

Catching the sound of a sob, to spare her further unhappi-
ness, I made it my business to stride loudly towards them, as
if I'd but just entered the corridor. Soon we were on our way,
a dismal little procession, to the place where Molly said she
read. Sure enough, a volume of Richardson's *Pamela* had a
feather between its leaves to mark the place.

Voke took the volume, and lent as she must have done
against a sturdy shelf. He looked up, and smiled. 'You could
have seen anyone touching that there picture that's gone,
couldn't you, Molly?'

She nodded silently.

'But you wouldn't dare tell Mr Dawson here or Mrs Lacock
lest they asked what you'd been doing in the library when you
were supposed to be beating carpets or fetching and carrying.
Now, Molly, weather apart, why were you afraid for the young
reverend's safety as he set off on the Haldon road – always
assuming it was the Haldon road, and you weren't trying to
put us off the scent?'

Mutely she shook her head, her eyes awash again.

'Now, my way of thinking is that this young reverend saw
you reading. Was he kind to you, or did he make you fearful?'

'Sort of both, Mr Voke.'

'Both? How can that be?'

'He gave me a guinea. And he promised to keep my secret
if I kept his. That he kept on coming back to see the picture
of the man and the woman.'

'But I think someone else came to see it too? Keeping a
quiet eye on Dr Shaldon?'

'He wrote in a book, Mr Voke.'

'He being Signor Polpetti?'

She nodded. 'And then I was worried, because he didn't write funny, like I thought Italian would be. He wrote in English.'

I gaped.

But Voke simply said kindly, 'Good girl. Now, my girl, are you sure it was the Haldon road this young reverend was heading for?' Turning to me he added, 'So who is pursuing whom? Which man is the thief, eh, Mr Dawson, and which the thief-catcher?'

Mrs Lacock and I felt we deserved a little of His Grace's Madeira wine when we sat together that evening, Mr Voke joining us, though in courtesy to Mrs Lacock he retired outside to smoke his filthy pipe. It had been a long hard day, but we flattered ourselves we had carried it off so well that none of the guests knew that anything had occurred to upset the even tenor of the hall. The picture was back in place, and Badger, the head keeper, had arrived in time to assist the unarmed Signor Polpetti when Dr Shaldon turned his pistols on him. When he realized his game was up, Dr Shaldon took the only path open to a gentleman wishing to prevent disgrace staining his family's escutcheon – he turned the pistol on himself.

After a few minutes' discussion, Mr Voke and Badger agreed that it might well be that in the thick mist he might have taken his pursuers for footpads, and, drawing his weapon, had mistakenly fired it as his horse reared, the bullet finding his own brain. A few guineas from His Grace's purse would ensure that the story became the official one. Only part of the truth would find its way into Signor Polpetti's notebook – a Bow Street Runner's Occurrence book. It seemed that many establishments like ours had lost works of art after one of his visits, and the most recent victim had set the Runners after him.

A few more guineas found their way to Molly, for her timely confession. Mrs Lacock was inclined to demur at that, but Mr Voke pointed out that without the girl's ultimate honesty, the picture would have disappeared into the mists and been lost for ever. But Mrs Lacock was adamant that she must find employment elsewhere, and I could not argue. A maid was supposed to be a maid, not a secret student.

So as we drank our Madeira, we discussed Molly's future. She was not qualified to be a governess, Mrs Lacock mused, and I had seen enough of the miseries attendant on a governess's life not to argue. Neither did I like Mrs Lacock's suggestion that she should seek a place for her as an old lady's maid-companion: Molly deserved the chance of a bit of life and a handsome young man to share it with.

At last, Mr Voke spoke up.

'I have a cousin down Okehampton way,' he began, 'who runs a small school for the daughters of farmers and so on; she might, if she were given a suitable premium, offer young Molly a place. The maiden could earn her keep as a maid-of-all-work, and learn as she went. In time she might become a pupil teacher, and better.'

'Yes, indeed,' Mrs Lacock cried. 'Who knows what a bright girl like that might achieve in time?'

But I nodded more slowly, with a sudden pang coming from I know not where.

TOGETHER IN ELECTRIC DREAMS
Carol Anne Davis

Carol Anne Davis has written a number of short stories in addition to five novels, including *Shrouded*. In recent years, she has also focused on writing about real-life crime, and her six titles include *Parents Who Kill*.

From the start, I did everything in my power to split them up, to make him exclusively mine again. But the bitch just wouldn't let go, so I was driven to kill. The psychologist here at the prison thinks that I overreacted, but she clearly hasn't loved enough . . .

I met him, of all places, on a sponsored walk for breast cancer. Both his mother and mine had died of the disease and it created an immediate bond between us. We were both forty, both divorced, both had one grown-up child who lived far away. Even our names sounded good together – Jack and Gill. My work as the assistant headmistress at a girls' school brought me into contact with very few men and his job as an aeronautics engineer meant that he worked with very few women. Neither of us had been dating for years so we were ready for action, fell hard.

Jack praised everything about me at the start – my looks, my figure, my somewhat dry sense of humour. He said that I was cute, that he loved my body, that I was very entertaining and that he loved spending time with me. I reciprocated with ardour, forever hugging and kissing him. He was always freshly showered and sweet-scented, so there was nothing that I wouldn't do . . .

And, at the onset, it seemed enough. He appeared to set out his stall, telling me that, if he remarried, his wife would get his sizeable pension. He was disappointed that his first wife had had so little interest in his work. Many women hear the word 'engineer' and turn away – they want a man with a job which they can understand, someone in sales or teaching. But I'd had friends in the engineering faculty when I studied English at university, simply because one of my sister's boyfriends was an engineer.

Throughout my course, I came to know these youths well, found that, if you looked beyond the initial awkwardness, they had good hearts and grounded personalities. They wanted what we all want, love and mutual support. They were the type of men who would hold their beloved in high esteem and would never cheat. Or so I thought . . .

I remember the first time I knew that something wasn't right. I'd been dating Jack for six months, and we were in love, when he went on one of his regular work nights out. By then, I'd met and socialized with most of his colleagues. Indeed, I often picked him up from the pub at the end of these evenings, sometimes joining him for the final round. But, on this particular evening, he was vague about exactly where they were going and said that he'd get a lift back from a mate.

The following day, I asked him which of the usual suspects were there. He reeled off a few names, hesitated, said, 'Becky', then added another few male names.

'Becky?' I asked. I mean, women in engineering are rarer than hen's teeth or at least they were when I was at uni.

'Mm, she joined us about a month ago.'

'Any good?' There had been one female engineer on my sister's boyfriend's course and she'd only survived by getting various blokes to help her with her course work. She was beauty without the brains. Her father had persuaded her to try engineering as she was his only child and he needed someone to take over the family firm.

'Yeah, she's OK.'

We were curled up on the settee and I'd just switched on the television and was about to leaf through the TV magazine. All of a sudden he was staring intently at the screen, yet it was showing *EastEnders*, a programme we both despised.

'There's a documentary just starting on BBC4,' I muttered, picking up the remote control but still watching him out of the corner of my eye.

'I'll make us a cuppa,' he said and catapulted off the couch.

I felt a growing unease as I waited for him to return. He'd always told me that he was a one-woman man and had given me no reason to doubt him. But the way he'd hesitated before mentioning her name . . .

'So, what does Becky do?' I asked when he returned with two overfilled mugs.

'She works for me.'

'Did she come from Ashtons?' I knew that another engineering firm had recently paid off their staff and that several of them had been taken on by the company which employed Jack.

'No, she's straight out of university.'

'A mere foetus!' I laughed, and waited for him to say that she was hopelessly callow.

Instead, he merely muttered, 'She's OK.'

It would be a month before I saw them together but I knew that she was my rival long before that. Put bluntly, he changed, became more distant. He stopped holding my hand when we were out walking and he went from greeting me with a 'Hi gorgeous' to a mere 'Hi'. He also started to find fault with my appearance, pinching my waistline and asking if I'd gained weight. Ironically, I'd lost a few pounds as I was terrified of losing him, was often too upset to eat.

I decided to go to the gym and tone up, though it was a horrible thought after a day spent dealing with overwrought teachers, pushy parents and hormonal pupils. But I was suddenly competing with a girl of twenty-two.

What with skipping meals and working out on the ski machine after school, I went from a size fourteen to a twelve in a fortnight. Then I waited outside Jack's work one day and saw him leave, laughing, with Becky and she must have been a perfect ten. She had long blonde tresses which caught the light and danced around in the summer breeze – mine's a brunette pixie cut and I have my share of bad hair days. She also had the straight white teeth of an American actress, whereas I have molars courtesy of the NHS.

It hurts to get your teeth straightened. It really does. They play that part down when you go for a private consultation.

Instead, they take your photo and show you what you're going to look like after your pegs are realigned. I signed up there and then and spent the next four months in pain, and still have ongoing discomfort. But they did look better, they really did. Even Jack said so, but he still didn't want me to pick him up from his work nights out.

I was getting slimmer, prettier, fitter, yet it wasn't enough. 'It's surprising that you still get spots at your age,' he said one day. In the bathroom a moment later, I looked in the mirror at the small red bump next to my gloss-enhanced lips and marvelled that my future happiness could depend on it. Dermabrasion helped, as did a lighter foundation, but I began to dread the run-up to my period when my complexion would be at its worst.

If you're a feminist, I bet that, by now, you're urging me to leave. And I should have done, I know, but he'd been so wonderful to me at the beginning. I kept thinking that, if I tried hard enough, I could get the man who had loved me back. I mean, it's not as if he was nasty all the time – he still took me out three times a week and made love to me as if he really meant it. And he still made future plans.

So, for the first eight months after Becky arrived, I convinced myself that he merely had a crush on her, that it wasn't reciprocated. After all, what would a twenty-two-year-old blonde beauty see in a forty-two-year-old man who was beginning to lose his hair?

She saw something, the bitch – maybe it was the thought of his pension or maybe she had a thing about father figures. Who knows? All I can say for sure is that I followed them from work one night and saw them go into an Italian restaurant. No boss. No colleagues. Just him and her, with their arms around each other's waists as they walked along the road and disappeared into The Venetian. I stood outside for a moment, feeling ill and afraid.

At first, I resolved not to mention it. I mean, what if he wanted to finish with me but just didn't have the guts? I'd be making it so easy for him to bring things to a swift conclusion. Instead, I decided just to hang on in there in the hope that she would find a guy of her own age and he'd return all of his affection to me.

My resolve lasted for two whole days then I burst into tears.

'What's wrong? You're usually so calm,' he said, taking his hand from my left breast where he'd been sending thrill after thrill through my nipple.

'I saw you holding hands with a blonde girl.'

'Christ,' he said, looking shocked, 'I never wanted you to know.'

I took a deep breath. 'I thought that we promised to be exclusive?'

He swallowed visibly. 'We did.'

'So?' *Don't end it, don't end it, don't end it.*

'She . . . she's just so young and lively. She really gets under my skin. But at the same time, she can be overwhelming. I love being with you as it's so nice and restful here.'

He made me sound like a day spa, but it was a start.

'At her age, her hormones must be all over the place?' I hoped against hope that she had wicked PMS.

'Tell me about it. For one week out of every month she snaps my head off and sometimes throws things at me!'

'And is that what you want?'

He shook his head. 'It's exhausting. But the rest of the time, she's . . .' He seemed to belatedly realize who he was talking to. 'I'm sorry, but she's really gotten to me.'

'It's probably just lust,' I said, trying to keep my voice from breaking again.

He shrugged. 'Who knows? Maybe I'm having an early midlife crisis.'

I tensed every sinew in my body. 'I'd like you to give her up.'

'I can't.'

'But we were so good together!'

'We still are. I don't want to lose either of you.'

I took the deepest of breaths. 'And if I issued an ultimatum?'

He looked down and played absently with my pubic hair. 'I'd choose her.'

So, there it was.

'Because she's new?'

'And different to everyone else that I've ever gone out with.

I mean, my wife and girlfriends have always been traditionalists.'

'But you are, too.'

'I was, but she's made me think about things differently. She's sort of New Age but she's somehow tied it all in with quantum mechanics. It's fascinating stuff.'

'I was something of a hippy at university,' I said, somewhat desperately. In other words, I'd owned a couple of tie dye outfits and an afghan coat.

'She likes all these esoteric things, believes in the supernatural.'

'But you're an atheist. We both are!'

'I think that I'd consider myself an agnostic nowadays.'

I should end this, I thought, then breathed in his aftershave and faint manly sweat and knew that I couldn't. I wanted him in my bed and in my life every single day. Surely three days a week was much, much better than nothing? He made me laugh, made me think, made me orgasm twice in one night. She was offering the hurly-burly of the futon whilst I gave him the deep, deep peace of the king-size bed.

I made the next three months so peaceful that it's a wonder he didn't die of bliss. We had once-weekly home-cooked meals at my place, washed down by the finest wines and brandies. We lay in my Jacuzzi and listened to whale music, made love using a vibrating relaxing massager which I'd purchased online. On other nights, we went to see feel-good movies or enjoyed weekend trips to bird sanctuaries and nature reserves.

Would he really enjoy going clubbing with her once the novelty had worn off? Was being the oldest swinger in town truly his preference? Surely he'd tire of her monthly aggression and choose comparatively laid-back me?

'Shall we go to the Eden Project this weekend?' I asked. Eve had tempted Adam with an apple but I was using greenery and pastoral music as my offerings.

'Can't – Becky's no longer going to her parents at the weekend so I'll be taking her dancing instead.'

I felt as if I'd been hit.

'What's changed?'

'They've moved abroad.'

'But she'd been seeing them every weekend?' I'd always thought that he mainly saw her straight from work, that he'd made an active choice to spend every Saturday and Sunday with me.

'Uh huh. They were running a struggling bed and breakfast and she was helping out.'

'So now you're going to switch between the two of us?'

He looked away then mumbled, 'Not sure.'

'What if she has PMS?'

'Oh, she's switched to a different pill. She's much better.'

'Is she really?' I said, and a little acid came back up from my stomach and burned my throat.

Have you any idea how difficult it is to fill an entire weekend when you know that the man you love is having fun with your much younger rival? Oh, I resurrected my old social life with the hillwalking club and went for meals out with my neighbour, but nothing brought me pleasure any more. Now I lived for Monday, Wednesday and Friday nights which I spent with Jack, sometimes socializing and sometimes staying in. I tried so hard to please him on these nights – my conversation sweet, my laughter ready, my tongue bionic – but he still went to her every weekend and maybe even saw her on Tuesdays and Thursdays too. Plus they were together all day at work, had hours in which to build up shared jokes. I couldn't compete.

Eventually, it began to affect my health so badly that I'd lie there in the mornings unable to get out of bed. I felt literally weighted. This was particularly strange as by now I'd lost two stone, looked pale and weak. I also lost concentration when I did finally arrive at work, was called in front of the board of governors and warned that I had to shape up. But he was still touching her, licking her, doing all of the things that he was doing to me but doubtless preferring her silkier and perkier body. It was driving me mad.

After the sacking, I signed on but the Job Centre didn't offer a new start.

'Once you're over forty . . .' one of the other jobseekers said sadly.

'Everything's aimed at people in their twenties,' I said savagely.

She had it all. I had less and less. We were reaching a showdown. It was then that I realized I had to kill.

It wasn't difficult. After all, I knew where they worked and lived, their day-to-day movements. I simply aimed my car and watched the body fly through the air. Afterwards, I ran over the cadaver as it lay on the ground, reversed and ran over it again numerous times. I was taking no chances, had to eliminate every breath.

I received a life sentence for his murder, of course. Does that surprise you? I mean, that it was Jack that I killed, my beloved? It surprised the prison psychologist.

'Why didn't you kill Becky, your rival?' she asked.

'Because there are new female graduates going into engineering all the time nowadays,' I said sadly, remembering my recent research. 'There would always be other young women tempting him away.'

'So why not let him go?'

'I loved him too much, he meant everything to me. This way he's mine for ever. No one else can ever have him now.'

'But you've given up everything in the process,' she said sadly.

I was so glad that she cared.

She's right though – life can be pointless in here unless you have someone to think about all of the time. Fortunately I realized within days that she and I are meant to be together. We talk easily during our sessions and she always looks pained when she admits that our time is up. She, too, used to work in an all-girls school so we share a history. I imagine she's also had secret crushes on the older girls, just like me. And there's a synchronicity in our names – she's Lilian and, if I use my full moniker, I'm Gillian. It's rhyme and reason. It's fate.

There's only one problem: Raisa, who is on the extended privileges programme, likes Lilian too. She has more independence than me as she's a trusted prisoner, has free reign of the building. She's probably popping in to see Lilian whilst I'm in the workshop, stuffing soft toys.

Not for much longer, though. I've bought a knife from one of the metal shop workers, had it honed to the sharpest point imaginable. I reckon it'll only take thirty seconds, during my one-to-one therapy, to cut the psychologist's throat. Lilian will always endure in my memory, alongside Jack, and neither of them will ever again be unfaithful. It's the ultimate ownership – I take their lives and they become mine.

SQUEAKY

Martin Edwards

Martin Edwards is the author of eight books featuring Liverpool lawyer Harry Devlin, as well as of the Lake District Mysteries, most recently *The Hanging Wood*. His stand-alone mysteries include *Dancing for the Hangman*, a novel about Dr Crippen. He has written many short stories, and 'The Bookbinder's Apprentice' won the CWA Short Story Dagger in 2008.

'*Let's go into the forest*,' Squeaky said.

Adele glanced at Brendan. Her husband was hunched over the steering wheel, eyes fixed on the road ahead. Lips motionless. She looked over her shoulder.

Squeaky squatted on the back seat, grinning at her.

Something about Squeaky disturbed Adele, and in wilder moments, she fancied Squeaky knew it. Those widely spaced blue eyes weren't as innocent as they ought to be. They stared through Adele, as if her skull were made of glass, exposing her thoughts like scrawl on a postcard.

The car rounded a bend. Fields dusted with the first snow of winter bordered either side of the road. In the distance, a dark gathering of trees stretched as far as she could see. A brown signpost for tourists pointed the way, but the lane was deserted.

'*Let's go into the forest.*'

The scratchy, high-pitched voice made Adele's flesh tingle. She clenched her small fists. Brendan's lips were parted. She could see the pink tip of his tongue. The car jerked forward, as he pressed his foot on the accelerator. They raced past the road sign.

'*But I wanted to go into the forest.*'

'Shut up!' Adele muttered.

'*Oh, dear me!*' This was Squeaky's catchphrase.

'I told you to shut up!'

How shaming, to scream like that at Squeaky. Stupid and immature of her, too, but she couldn't help herself. Brendan threw her a glance. Was that dread in his eyes? The heater was buzzing – he had changed it to the highest setting – and the car's interior was stuffy. Sweat slicked his brow.

'Are you . . . OK?' His voice never used to falter like this.

'Fine,' she said. 'Yeah, I'm fine.'

They drove on in silence for another twenty minutes, until they reached the hospice on the outskirts of the next town. While Brendan waited to reverse into a vacant space, Adele jumped out to buy a parking ticket. She took another look at Squeaky through the window of the car. Snub-nosed and straw-haired, with a red top and baggy blue jeans. A figure that might have walked out of a bad dream. Squeaky ought to find it impossible to scare a grown woman. But a tremor ran down Adele's spine as she shoved coins into the slot of the machine.

When she returned to stick the ticket on to the windscreen, Brendan had Squeaky over his shoulder, and the big canvas hold-all in his hand. He pecked Adele on the cheek.

'See you later . . . Have a good shop.'

Why couldn't he meet her eye? She strove for brightness. 'Good luck. Hope the kids have a wonderful time.'

As she walked towards the main road, Squeaky's piercing gaze seemed to track her movements. She felt naked, despite being wrapped against the cold in a warm woollen coat and scarf. Squaring her shoulders, she looked straight ahead, determined not to spare Squeaky another glance. Though she itched to put her hands round that scrawny neck.

Drifting through the crowds in the shopping mall, she found it impossible to push Squeaky out of her mind. Sometimes she thought there were three people in their marriage, not two. Whenever she tried to talk about her anxieties to Brendan, he was kind but intransigent. Squeaky had changed his life for the better, he said. Surely Adele understood? He'd found his true vocation. It wasn't as if his wife had any cause to worry.

After all, Squeaky was only a doll.

*   *   *

When Adele first met Brendan, at a party thrown by a casual acquaintance neither of them knew well or much liked, he told her he was a magician. After their first night in bed together, he confessed that his magic amounted to little more than a few conjuring tricks. He didn't even run to a glamorous assistant, he said with a mock-sheepish grin. For years, he'd worked as a quantity surveyor, but after the death of his wife he'd wanted to change his life completely. Adele knew how he felt.

They had plenty in common. Liked the same TV shows, laughed at the same jokes. He was marvellous company, charming and courteous, although Adele was perceptive enough to detect a streak of self-indulgence running through him. But that had been true of Josh, it was true of most men. Maybe all men. Brendan was a nice guy, but not the strongest of characters; forced into a corner, he'd put himself first. But you had to balance positives against the negatives. Brendan made her smile, for the first time since Josh's accident, when they were out boating in his native Australia, on the final day of the holiday of a lifetime to celebrate their fifth wedding anniversary.

Bereavement was another thing they had in common. Brendan made no secret of his devotion to the first Mrs O'Leary. Not that Adele resented this: jealousy wasn't one of her vices. She deplored the way Gilly had betrayed Brendan's trust. He still kept photos of her in an old suitcase in the loft, and the identical pout featured in every single one. Gilly was pretty and vain, the doted-on daughter of a widowed wealthy banker. When Daddy died, she needed someone else to spoil her rotten. It was clear even from Brendan's kind-hearted comments that she'd been flattered by his unfailing attentiveness, and relished having a good-looking man at her beck and call. And Brendan, tall and introspective, with a mop of dark hair and deep brown eyes, was a very good-looking man.

Adele lingered in her favourite fashion store, where Christmas carols sung by a kids' choir trilled over the loudspeakers.

'Brightly shone the moon that night
Though the frost was cruel.'

After that disturbing episode with Squeaky, she was in

the mood for a treat. A skimpy designer nightdress caught her eye. The price was extortionate for something so skimpy and insubstantial, but money wasn't a problem, and Brendan would love slipping it off her slim white shoulders. So, a treat for both of them. She carried her trophy to the till.

Poor Brendan deserved his fun. He was terrific in bed, but that hadn't been enough for vain and selfish Gilly. She'd started an affair with an old school friend called Hodgkinson, who'd contacted her via a social networking site. Hodgkinson was married to a woman disabled by some rare malfunction of her auto-immune system. Brendan knew none of this until the police came knocking at his door one Saturday afternoon, and told him that his wife had been found dead in a car filled with exhaust fumes. She and the school friend had perpetrated the ultimate in selfishness. A suicide pact.

'*Sire, the night is darker now*
And the wind blows stronger
Fails my heart, I know not how,
I can go no longer.'

She stabbed her PIN number into the credit card machine. Brendan was quite open about the fact that the police had needed to check him out in order to make sure that he hadn't contrived an ingenious double murder. To a suspicious detective, the affair might seem to give him a motive to do away with Gilly and her lover, and to make matters worse, Brendan inherited all the money her father had left her.

Lucky he was a conjuror in his spare time. While Gilly spent her last hours with her lover, he'd risen bright and early to travel to a hotel in Bath where he'd been booked by a distant cousin to perform some table magic at her husband's fortieth birthday party.

It all made sense. Gilly was a flake, the other man was depressed about his wife's deteriorating health, and they couldn't see a happy future together. Two star-crossed lovers whose self-absorption knew no bounds.

And even if a suicide pact seemed an overreaction, what other explanation could there be? The lover's wife was immobile in a hospital bed, while Brendan had a perfect alibi.

*   *   *

It was so sad. Brendan explained to Adele that after Gilly's death, somehow he couldn't face performing magic tricks any more. She sympathized; he was a sensitive soul. The money he inherited enabled him to pack up his job, but he still yearned to become an entertainer. Six months after he and Adele returned home from a blissful honeymoon cruise in the Caribbean, he stumbled across an internet auction that seized his imagination.

Squeaky was for sale.

As a schoolboy, he told Adele, he'd practised mimicry from time to time, but magic was his first love. On the spur of the moment, he decided to acquire a dummy of his own and become a ventriloquist.

At first, Adele was delighted. Brendan needed to scrub the memory of magic – and Gilly's treachery – out of his mind. What better way than to discover a fresh interest? For a few weeks, because they believed in sharing, she even taught herself ventriloquism. Its mysterious nature intrigued her; the first ventriloquists had been shamans and gastromancers, and the idea of taking on another persona seemed attractive.

'You've got a knack for it!' he'd exclaimed in delight.

She'd tried to look modest. 'I just believe a couple ought to share their interests, that's all.'

All too soon, the novelty palled. As it did, she found herself disliking Squeaky more with every week that passed. How silly, to loathe a stuffed dummy. Yet she couldn't help feeling dismayed by the amount of time Brendan devoted to his hobby. Worse, he teased her by making Squeaky poke fun at her clothes and hairstyles. All in good spirit, of course, but Squeaky's sense of humour was sharper and less kindly than Brendan's. Once or twice, a barbed jest got under Adele's skin.

Was Squeaky a boy or a hoydenish girl? Brendan was vague, and the dummy's appearance and voice were oddly sexless. But there was no denying that Squeaky had a spiky personality, tainted by malevolence. He, she or it – whatever – seemed to glory in stirring up trouble.

Before long, Adele wanted Squeaky out of the house, but Brendan was better at ventriloquism than he'd even been at magic, and he wouldn't hear of ditching the dummy. He started to pick up bookings: children's birthday parties, in the main, but he also performed in social clubs and rest homes. Today he was putting on a show for sick children in a hospice. Brightening their troubled lives.

When Adele pushed it, they had their first blazing row. Brendan's pleasant face turned pink with outrage. He wouldn't hear of getting rid of Squeaky. How could Adele possibly make a fuss about a doll who brought pleasure to countless people, kids and old folk in particular?

Adele found herself shouting, 'Sometimes I think you care more about that fucking dummy than you do about me!'

'You're making a fool of yourself,' he hissed. 'Behaving like a spoiled brat.'

He'd never criticized her before, and that came as such a shock, in the end she gave in. Usually, Brendan was master of his emotions. But she'd seen something new in him. A cussed determination that was proof against anything she might say. She saw that he found her objections to Squeaky mean-spirited and neurotic.

Shopping done, she decided a quick gin and tonic would fortify her for the return trip with Squeaky. She wasn't due to meet up with Brendan for another half hour, so she made her way to The Spread Eagle, on the other side of the road from the hospice. It wasn't a salubrious locality, and the pub didn't have a good reputation, but who cared? Suppose some man chatted her up, she wouldn't start kicking and screaming. She could do with being made to feel good. To feel herself desired again.

Walking up to the bar, she glanced in a large oval mirror that hung above the counter. In the reflection, she saw Brendan. He was seated at a table, with a half-pint glass of beer in front of him, handing a padded envelope to a bulky man with a broken nose.

For God's sake. It was Gerard Finucane.

Adele didn't wait to be served. As Finucane put the envelope in the jacket of his coat, she turned on her heel and hurried out into the wintry evening.

*   *   *

Waiting in the car, Adele realized she'd have minded less if she'd caught Brendan groping a busty barmaid. Gerard Finucane was bad news. And wasn't he supposed to have gone back to Ireland after the trial?

Finucane was a builder, and Brendan knew him through work. They were friends, but made an odd couple, a quiet and nervy professional and a loud, egotistical extrovert. Finucane called himself an entrepreneur, but that was simply a synonym for a criminal. Brendan introduced Adele to him before the wedding, and when they went out for a drink as a threesome, she realized within minutes that this was a man who loved taking risks. He didn't care, he simply couldn't help himself. Brazenly, he stroked her leg under the table while Brendan told a tedious anecdote about some job they'd worked on together. For a few minutes, she did nothing about it, but when Finucane's fingers strayed under the hem of her skirt, she gave him a fierce look and shifted her chair away. His response was a cheeky wink and an excessively loud guffaw when Brendan belatedly delivered an anticlimactic punchline.

Finucane hadn't made it to the wedding, because he'd been remanded in custody, accused along with a couple of thugs who worked for him of beating up a business rival and leaving him brain-dead. Reluctantly, Brendan admitted to Adele that Finucane had been inside more than once in his life. But the trial folded on the first day when the main prosecution witnesses failed to turn up. Had they been threatened? Nothing could be proved. Finucane and his henchmen walked away from court without a stain on their characters.

Even so. How could a decent, caring man like Brendan be friendly with a violent criminal like Gerard Finucane?

And what was inside the padded envelope?

'How was your afternoon?'

'Oh, it was great. The kids loved Squeaky.'

Nothing much else was said on the way home. No mention of a trip to The Spread Eagle, though Adele's nostrils detected a beery whiff. Squeaky uttered not a word, but when Adele stole a glance at the back seat, Squeaky's grin seemed as triumphant as it was vindictive.

Brendan and Adele lived in a split-level house on a steep hill overlooking a fast-flowing stream. It was a new-build and obtaining planning permission in the green belt had been fraught with problems, but Brendan knew the right people and, for all Adele knew, greased the right palms. She didn't care if a few rules needed to be bent; their new home occupied one of the most desirable locations in the north of England, and when it was finished it would be worth a fortune. A balcony was to be built on to the living room, from which in summer they would be able to look down on the stream and the woods beyond.

Before getting married, they'd talked about starting a family. Adele liked the idea of having kids; Josh hadn't been interested, but something was lacking in her life and she wondered if it might be motherhood. Not that she was starry-eyed about small children; she'd taken an unpaid position as a classroom assistant in a school in the next village, and she found the constant squabbling a bore. But you saw your own offspring differently from other people's.

A month ago, she had told Brendan she'd stopped taking her contraception, but since the row about Squeaky, they hadn't made love. Brendan wasn't a man for reconciliation sex – quite a contrast to Josh, and one of the few areas where the comparison favoured her first husband – and she was becoming frustrated by his continued lack of response. She had her needs, and one of the things that had most attracted her to Brendan had been his skill at fulfilling them.

'Shall we open a bottle of Chablis?' she asked before starting the meal. 'I need a drink, how about you?'

Brendan frowned. He was fussy about mixing the grape and the grain. Now was the moment for him to mention that he'd had a quick half and a catch-up with Gerard Finucane.

He cleared his throat. 'Lovely. I could do with a drop of alcohol myself. I love performing for an audience, but it does leave me shattered.'

As they were undressing in their vast and luxurious bedroom that night, Brendan launched into a long and complicated explanation about the delay to the building of the balcony and the garage block. Adele hated mess, and yearned for the work to be finished. She was almost tempted to ask if he should bring Finucane in to speed it up. For all his faults, at least Finucane was renowned for getting things done.

Adele lay in bed, waiting for her husband. He took an age cleaning his teeth. Did he want her to give up and fall asleep with boredom? She decided to go on to the offensive.

'Why did you let Squeaky talk like that in the car?'

Through the open door to the en suite bathroom, she saw Brendan freeze in the act of lifting his electric toothbrush.

'Just leave it, can you, please?'

'Brendan, I'm trying to help.

'You're not helping,' he muttered.

'Why did Squeaky want to go into the forest?'

He spat into the basin and padded back towards their king-size bed. She saw that he'd developed some sort of tic in his left eye. Nerves? What did he have to be stressed about?

'I don't want to talk about it.'

He clambered into bed and she stretched an arm around his waist.

'Brendan, it's not natural. We both know what happened in the forest. Why are you letting that bloody doll talk like that? What's going on?'

He lifted a hand and switched off the light. They never made love in the dark, she didn't know why. Her guess was that Gilly had preferred it with the lights out, and this was one of the changes Brendan had made in his life. New woman, new house, new adventures in the bedroom. He'd been so inventive, until the arrival of Squeaky.

'Goodnight.'

'Brendan, we need to discuss this.'

He wriggled out of her grip and did not reply.

'Brendan.'

No answer. Was he trembling? And if so, why?

'*Let's go into the forest.*'

Adele woke in the early hours, hearing Squeaky's voice in her head. As a rule she was a sound sleeper; even when Josh died, she'd kept managing to get six or seven hours each night.

The forest meant only one thing to Brendan. Among the oaks and the firs was the lay-by where Gilly and her boyfriend had parked their car, not far from the cottage where the lover lived, before poisoning themselves with exhaust fumes.

Brendan was snoring. The sleep of the just? Adele couldn't help doubting it.

Was he giving money to Finucane in that padded envelope, and if so, why was payment due? Time to think the unthinkable. Suppose that, instead of being in Dublin, Finucane had sneaked back into England, and killed Gilly and the man on Brendan's behalf. He was capable of murder, but surely Brendan wasn't? Not Brendan, the charming, introspective worrier she had fallen in love with.

Yet he had a powerful double motive. What if greed and jealousy had driven him to do something terrible – or rather, hire Finucane to do something terrible, and now he was tormented by guilt?

That might explain an obsession with the two deaths in that fume-filled car, and Squeaky's insistent demand.

'Let's go into the forest.'

No! There was a flaw in the theory. Relief flooded through her. Finucane was streetwise, in a way Brendan never could be. If Finucane had agreed to carry out a couple of contract killings, he'd have insisted on payment in advance. Or, at the least, half his money upfront, half on delivery of his side of the bargain. Inconceivable that he'd have waited until now to take his money. Brendan couldn't have been paying him for services rendered. Maybe there was something other than cash in the envelope, maybe . . .

Another thought struck her, and even snuggled under the thick duvet, she found herself shivering.

What if he wanted Finucane to undertake another job for him?

'Where's Squeaky?' Brendan demanded the next morning.

They were breakfasting in their magnificent new kitchen. Through the panoramic windows, Adele watched tentative snowflakes drift on to the York stone flags before melting.

'More toast?'

'Did you hear me?' Brendan's voice rose as he struggled to control his emotions. 'What have you done with Squeaky?'

'Wouldn't you like to know?'

A good impersonation, even if Adele said so herself. Her lips didn't move at all, and she thought she'd captured Squeaky's provocative, malicious tone.

Brendan slipped off the high stool and advanced towards her. His eyes shone with anger, his shoulders were rigid with tension.

'For God's sake, what have you done?'

'Oh, dear me!'

Adele had climbed out of bed in the middle of the night, taken Squeaky from the bed in the room next door to theirs, and hidden the doll in a linen basket in the utility room. The temptation to throw Squeaky in the dustbin, or even go outside and toss it down into the stream, had almost overpowered her. Yet somehow she'd kept calm enough to resist the urge to be rid of Squeaky for ever.

And it was worth the effort, to see the truth revealed in Brendan's eyes.

He cared more for Squeaky than he did for her.

A week later, Adele was sitting in a restaurant, enjoying a turkey dinner with colleagues from the school where she worked, when a discreet waiter asked her to accompany him to the manager's office. There she found a young woman police officer with sorrowful eyes and a bad case of acne.

'Mrs Keane?'

'Yes, what is it?'

'I'm so sorry to interrupt your Christmas meal. Would you like to sit down, please?'

The restaurant manager, face etched with anxiety, pulled out a chair for her.

'What's happened?'

'I'm afraid I have some bad news for you.'

Adele counted the pimples on the woman's cheeks. Said nothing.

'It's your husband. I'm sorry to say that he has been in an accident.'

'Oh my God. Is he hurt?'

The woman bowed her head. 'I'm afraid he died a short time ago.'

Adele made a small yelping noise of incoherent distress.

'I am so sorry, Mrs Keane.'

'What . . . what in Heaven's name happened?'

'He was hit by a motor vehicle as he left a public house.'

Adele stared. 'Yes, he told me he'd be popping out for a pint while I enjoyed myself with my friends.'

The woman cleared her throat. 'I have to tell you, the driver did not stop. We suspect he'd been drinking. There were eyewitnesses who said the vehicle swerved before it knocked down your husband, and then accelerated out of sight. The driver must have known he'd hit someone. But it's the time of year. In the run-up to Christmas, people drink far too much. It's appallingly irresponsible.'

'Nice place,' Finucane said a couple of nights later, as he looked around the living room. 'No expense spared.'

Adele was bored with playing the grieving widow. Putting her glass down on a glass-topped occasional table, she sat on the sofa and kicked off her shoes. 'Nothing but the best, was Brendan's motto. He had the money, and he didn't mind spending it.'

Finucane said something coarse about Brendan.

'I suppose we ought to talk about your fee,' Adele said.

Finucane grinned at her. 'You already made a payment in kind in the hotel, don't forget. I'm not some bog-standard mercenary, you know. We can come to an arrangement, you and me.'

Adele chortled and lifted her glass. 'Suits me, sweetie. So here's to . . . mutually satisfactory arrangements.'

He swallowed some wine and fingered the brickwork of the exposed chimney breast. 'Not bad,' he said, with deliberate ambiguity. 'Not bad at all.'

'I want to know about Gilly.'

He put a stubby finger to his lips. 'Ask no questions and I'll tell you no lies.'

'Come on, Ged. I'm dying to know the gory details. How did you do it?'

He laughed. 'You're really something, you know?'

'Yes, I do know. Satisfy my curiosity, and then we can finish the bottle upstairs.'

A theatrical sigh. 'Women, eh?'

'Can't live with them, can't live without them?'

A broad grin. He wasn't handsome, not in Brendan's league at all in terms of looks, but she was conscious of a crude magnetism pulling her towards him.

'All right, if you really must know. When Brendan was away, Gilly had the house to herself. Once her feller, Hodgkinson, left his wife in hospital, he came around. They had a few drinks and smoked some dope before going to bed. I was waiting for my chance.'

'Go on.' She saw he relished having an audience. A bit like Brendan with Squeaky.

'I fitted a garden hose that Brendan had left out for me to the exhaust of Gilly's estate car, using a kid's feeding bottle which he'd cut in half. Wearing surgical gloves, I ran the hose through the garage and utility room and up a hole in the floorboards right underneath the bed. As soon as I switched on the engine, I nipped upstairs. The two of them were dead to the world. I pulled the duvet over Hodgkinson's nose and mouth, squeezed hard for half a minute and pushed the hose into his face with my right hand, and held it there until he was dead. Same with Gilly, she was stoned, and barely struggled. Not that she was strong enough to fight back, even if she'd realized what was happening. She was a tiny, frail woman. Big tits, mind.'

'Not as nice as mine, though.'

'No way, darling, you're one of a kind.'

She licked her lips provocatively. 'You'd better believe it.'

'Anyway, I lugged both of them to the car and put them in the boot with a blanket over their heads. I'd put a folding bicycle in the car as well. After I'd driven to the forest, I dumped Hodgkinson in the driver's seat. Gilly stayed in the boot. I put some family photos that Brendan gave me next to her body, put earphones on her, and switched on her iPod, so it seemed she'd been listening to her favourite Leonard Cohen tracks. And then I connected a length of vacuum hose to the exhaust, put the other end in the boot, and switched on the ignition. Once the scene was set, I took out the bike and cycled away. We had a couple of lucky breaks. Hodgkinson had told his wife's nurse that he couldn't bear what was happening to her. She thought suicide was in his mind. And the detective leading the inquiry owed me a favour. Some of the forensic stuff was mislaid. Nothing could be proved.'

Adele clapped her hands. 'Amazing!'

He fondled her bare neck. 'Yeah, that's me. Amazing.'

'And it doesn't bother you? That you killed a couple?'

He exhaled. 'It was a job. You can't be sentimental.'

'Not like Brendan. His conscience bothered him.'

'Not enough to stop him wanting you out of the way, sweetheart. Lucky you realized and got in touch.'

'Lucky you were willing to change sides.'

A raucous laugh. 'No contest. I've always fancied you, Adele, you must know that.'

'I suppose so,' she said with a sweet smile.

'Brendan didn't know when he was well off.'

'No.' Adele ran her fingers through Finucane's hair. 'Did he say anything about this . . . new relationship?'

'Nah, he made a mystery out of it. Whoever he was seeing, I bet she didn't compare to you.'

Adele pictured Squeaky's weird eyes and red lips.

'You're right.'

Finucane closed his eyes as her hand slid between his legs.

'Ged, is that you?'

Finucane sat up with a start, swearing wildly.

'What was that?'

Adele moved away from him, gasping in fear. 'A voice . . . it sounded like . . . no, it can't be.'

'Some kind of joke?' Finucane swore again. 'You're not telling me Brendan's risen from the dead?'

'I think the voice came from outside.' Adele pointed to the sliding doors. They hadn't pulled the curtains when they came into the living room. Outside, the night was black. Not a star to be seen.

Finucane sprang to his feet. 'Some bastard spying on us? They'll be sorry.'

'Ged, be careful!'

'Don't worry.' He put his hand in his pocket and pulled out a small knife. 'Nobody messes me around.'

'I don't think I locked the doors,' she said in a whisper. 'He might . . . come in.'

'Switch the light off,' Finucane hissed.

With her finger on the switch, Adele said, 'What are you going to do?'

'What do you think?'

The last thing she saw before the light went out was the glint of the blade in his palm. She heard him pull at the handle of the sliding doors, and then move through them. Moments later came the scream.

'Oh, dear me!'

She just couldn't resist it, as she switched the lights back on. Walking to the open doors, she looked down at the concrete fifteen feet below. Finucane's body was a heap of broken bones. Better check to make sure he was dead before she called the police to tell them about the intruder who had threatened her with his knife before falling to his death, unaware that the sliding doors gave on to a balcony that did not exist. Adele didn't believe in taking chances.

Five minutes later, after dialling 999, she made her way upstairs and went into the spare room. Squeaky was lying on the bed, staring at her. At least, Adele said to herself, her ventriloquial skills had come in handy tonight. Only one thing left to do now. Was that fear in the doll's eyes? If not, it ought to be.

She tore the doll's head off, and then the rest of its limbs.

Yes, it was childish, but strangely satisfying. Certainly she didn't feel a twinge of remorse as she waited for the police to arrive. She'd never fretted about tipping Josh out of that boat, the day after he told her he wanted a divorce, and she wouldn't waste any tears on Brendan or Finucane, let alone horrid, ugly Squeaky.

Leave the guilt to her dead husband, and his dismembered conscience.

ALL THAT GLISTERS

Jane Finnis

Jane Finnis was born in Yorkshire, where she still lives. She developed an early fascination for Roman history, and studied history at London University. Her knowledge of the subject informs her four novels about life and death in first-century Britain; her latest title is *Danger in the Wind*.

'Tony, how good to see you. Come in, come in. It's been a long time. Too much water under the bridge.' That was typical of Giles – the expansive smile, the sincere cliché. 'We ought to have kept in touch, you know, we really ought.'

'Well, we're both busy people. "Time like an ever-rolling stream bears all its sons away . . ."' And that, I admit, was typical of me. I always avoid a direct lie when I can, and if I resort to a cliché, it's usually a quotation.

Giles laughed. 'Still quoting the classics, I see. Walking library, we used to call you, didn't we? Where's that one from – Shakespeare?'

'It's part of a hymn, you ignorant heathen.'

We both laughed then, and for a few moments it was as if we'd stepped back twenty years, to our schooldays and our friendship.

'Let's sit by the window,' Giles said. 'There's whisky on the table, or coffee if you prefer.'

I put my briefcase down carefully and sank into a leather armchair. 'What a stunning view! Nice office, too. You millionaires do yourselves pretty well.'

'No point earning it if you don't spend it.'

The office was like its owner, large and showy. It was on the thirtieth floor, with huge windows to make the most of the city panorama below. The furniture was antique, and the computers were state-of-the-art. The smell of money was everywhere.

'Thanks for coming,' he said as he sat down facing me.

'No problem. I was delighted when you rang me.' You bet I was. It had taken me several months to engineer this meeting. 'And flattered, too. There are several other experts you could have consulted.'

'Not in your league, Tony. You're flying as high in your chosen field as I am in mine.'

'Thanks.'

We drank – I stuck to coffee, Giles didn't – and exchanged banalities. I asked after his wife (number three to reach that elevation), and commented on his company's recent dramatic expansion into the Middle East. He congratulated me on my professorship, and complimented me on my latest television series about Iron Age Britain.

'Which brings us,' he said, 'to my reason for contacting you. Have you looked at it?'

'I have.' I took the cardboard box from my briefcase, and with a conjuror's flourish, unwrapped the shining object inside, and stood it carefully on the table.

It was about ten inches long, a model of an ancient boat; the kind of frail-looking craft made of wood and animal skins in which our Celtic ancestors sailed round the coasts of Britain two thousand years ago. The details were perfect – the mast, the rowers' benches, the oars, even an anchor, all done to scale.

And it was made entirely of gold.

I suppose some people would say an old boat wasn't an especially attractive subject, but to me it was wonderful, and I couldn't resist another quotation. '"It was so old a ship – who knows, who knows? And yet so beautiful . . ."'

He groaned. 'All right, all right. Shakespeare this time?'

'No. From a poem by James Elroy Flecker, early twentieth century.'

'Never heard of him. Now can we get to the point? What have you discovered?'

'You asked me,' I said slowly, 'to check out this little treasure, and confirm that it was made in the first century AD, or possibly the first century BC, as you were told by the man you bought it from.'

'He seemed honest enough, but he was only a student with a metal detector, not an expert. It's your opinion that counts. If it's genuine, it'll be worth a small fortune. Or even a large one.' He took a drink of whisky.

'Correct. So I've examined it extremely thoroughly. I ran tests to analyse the composition of the gold – I'm sure you know that even the purest gold contains other metals too. Silver, copper . . .'

'Yes, yes, I've done my homework. And I know you've been able to test it using X-rays and such, so you didn't have to harm the boat itself.'

'Correct again.'

'And your conclusion?'

'It's a fake.'

'A *fake*?' He stared at me. 'All that glitters is not gold, you mean? You see, I can throw in an appropriate quote too, if I have to.'

'Inappropriate, and incorrect anyway.' I grinned at him. 'First, because it *is* gold, and second, because what Shakespeare actually wrote was, "All that *glisters* is not gold".'

'Glitters, glisters, who cares, as long as it's the real thing?'

'Come on, you're not that naïve. The gold itself is OK. It could even have originated in Ireland, as you were told. But that boat wasn't made two thousand years ago. Not even two hundred years. Two, possibly.'

'How can you be so sure?'

'It's the style. It isn't – well, it isn't quite right for a Celtic boat of that period. It's hard to put into words, but I just *know* it isn't. It's the work of an excellent goldsmith, but if he lived in the Iron Age, I'm Julius Caesar. You bought it from a student, you say?'

'That's right. He said he found it in a bog somewhere in Ireland. He thought it was old and valuable, but was prepared to let it go cheap, because he was desperate for ready cash. You know how broke students always are.'

'I remember it well.' I'd been permanently broke at university, despite doing two part-time jobs during term time, and three in the so-called vacations. My mother couldn't have managed without my weekly contribution. Dad was dead, and we had my younger sister to support. I've got money now, but if you've ever gone through really hard times, you never forget.

Giles, on the other hand, always had money. He went straight from school into his father's flourishing engineering business, and was sent off to one of the Far Eastern factories to 'learn the ropes'. The only rope he'd never had to master was how to live solely on the wages his workers earned. Our boyhood friendship ended then, and I hadn't seen him since.

Giles leaned forward in his chair. 'You're quite sure about this, Tony? You wouldn't spin me a yarn?'

'Not even a golden one! Believe me, I wish I could say it's worth a million or three. Of course it'll fetch a bit, a nice piece like that, and perhaps I shouldn't have called it a fake – a reproduction, that sounds better.' I poured myself more coffee from the silver pot on the table, bending my head so he couldn't see my eyes.

When I looked up again, he was grinning broadly. 'I know that boat's not genuine first century.'

'Ah. You've had somebody else examine it?'

'I didn't need to. I've met the man who made it.'

'Have you indeed? Tell me more.'

'He lives in London, goes by the name of Jack Baker, although I think that's an alias of some kind, because he's got a hint of a continental accent. Anyway, he's a superb craftsman. He makes very expensive gold jewellery most of the time, that's how I found him, or rather my wife did. I've bought her several of his pieces, and got to know him personally. He told me that now and then he makes something a little different. And when he showed me this boat . . . well, we came up with an interesting idea.'

I waited like a fisherman feeling the first twitch at his line.

'I asked you to value the boat because I wanted to make sure we are still friends. I need a friend, someone I can trust, like in the old days.'

'The old days are gone, Giles. But I'm not going to tell you something is genuine when it's a fake, am I? Now if it was the other way round, of course . . .' I laughed. 'No, only kidding. You know me, I hate lying.'

'You always did. But sometimes it's necessary.'

'Sometimes, perhaps.'

'Do you remember what we used to say at school? We two must always stand together, or we'll fall apart.'

Even after twenty years, our old pledge of loyalty sent a shiver down my spine. We'd last spoken it on a summer night by a lake, while a beautiful girl lay dead on the grass between us.

It had been a dreamlike evening to start with, full of moonlight and even a nightingale's song. A picnic by the lake, just the three of us – Giles, me, and Lisette Boulanger, the prettiest girl in the school, as well as the most exotic: half-French, sexy as hell, and aloof as a snowbound alp. Every senior boy fancied her, and Giles and I had a bet that one of us would be first to win her. I started favourite, helped by my knowledge of poetry; but Giles could play the romantic too, and as the evening wore on, I couldn't tell for sure which of us she preferred. Probably she was just enjoying having two young men dancing attendance.

After the picnic, we rowed out on the water. We'd all had too much wine, and when Giles insisted on standing up in the stern to row, his clowning capsized us. We all laughed as we tumbled into the lake. We were strong swimmers and it wasn't far to the shore. Giles called, 'You two head for the bank. I'll push the boat back.'

That shows how drunk we were. None of us thought of righting the boat and clambering in again. The water wasn't cold, and the night air was so warm we'd soon be dry once we got to shore, especially if we took our wet clothes off and lay on the grass.

'Tony, Giles, help! Help me!' As I reached the bank I heard Lisette calling out. For a moment I didn't take it in, but when she shouted again I recognized panic in her voice, and I found I was suddenly sober. I couldn't see her in the moonlight so I listened, trying to pinpoint her direction, and she cried out yet again, desperate and shrill. I plunged back into the water and swam towards the sound of her voice.

I was too slow reaching her. She was barely conscious and

only just afloat. By the time I got her to the bank she wasn't breathing. I tried mouth-to-mouth resuscitation, and so did Giles when he reached us. She just lay there, still and staring.

Our panicky young voices resounded in my head, as they had so many times since:

'My God, Tony, look, she's dead!'

'But she was a good swimmer. I don't understand it.'

'I put something in her drink. Just a couple of pills. I never thought . . .'

'You spiked her drink, and then she couldn't swim? Giles, you killed her!'

'If anyone killed her it was you. You could have got to her quicker, but you weren't really trying because you were jealous . . .'

'Of course I tried, which is more than you did.'

Giles was the first to calm down. 'This is stupid. Nobody killed her, it was an accident. An accident, a dreadful accident. We must find a phone and call the police. We'll tell them exactly what happened, how the boat turned over, how we did our best to save her. But we didn't know she'd been taking pills. All right?'

'How could you do that to Lisette?'

'I've done it before with girls. I suppose I just didn't think.'

'You're still not thinking. We can't lie about something like this.'

'We can. We must. Whatever we do, it can't help Lisette now. There's bound to be an enquiry, and we've got to think about saving our own reputations.'

'Reputations? What do they matter?'

'Trust me, they matter. This was a tragic accident. All right?'

'Well . . . all right.'

'Listen, we two must always stand together, or we'll fall apart.'

I jolted back to reality to find Giles standing over me, holding out a tumbler of whisky. 'Drink this, you look as if you need it. What's up? Aren't you feeling well?'

'I'm OK. Just those old words, they took me right back to . . . you know.'

He nodded. 'Horrible. We were lucky to get away with it.'

'I still have nightmares about it sometimes.'

'Really? I can't say I think about it much.'

'I do. And about the police enquiries, and the papers . . . and my father so ashamed of me. Even though our story was believed, he said I'd disgraced the whole family.'

I finished the whisky and reached for my coffee cup, while Giles went calmly back to his chair. Could it be he hadn't realized the effect his words would have on me? Or did he know full well, and perhaps think he had some kind of hold over me? I had let him use me when we were kids, but it wouldn't happen again.

I focused my attention on the golden boat. 'Let's get back to the matter in hand. You were saying you and Baker had an interesting idea.'

'Can't you guess?'

I sipped my coffee in silence for a while, listening to the faraway sounds of London's traffic. 'He thought it could be a good enough reproduction to pass for genuine, and sell for a nice big price, but he couldn't sell it himself. He suggested you sell it for him, and the two of you split the take?'

He smiled his expansive smile. 'Got it in one, except there'd be three of us to share, if you come in with us.'

'*Me?*'

'We need you to certify that it's genuine. If you vouch for it, selling it will be a doddle.'

I shook my head. 'Sorry, it's far too risky. A sale like that would attract too much attention. The media would pick it up, and we couldn't prevent other experts from examining it. I'm not the only one who can spot reproduction Celtic art.'

'Now who's being naïve? I'm not suggesting we auction it at Sotheby's under the eyes of the world's television cameras. I'm thinking about a private sale to an art collector who'll accept your assurance that it's two thousand years old, and pay us the going rate. Why not?'

'I think "why?" is more important than "why not?". Why on earth are you even considering this? It's a hell of a risk, and you don't need the money, do you?'

'As it happens, I do. Can I tell you something in confidence?'

'We both know we're good at secrets.'

'I need an injection of cash for the business. I need it urgently, and I don't want to tell the world about it. You mentioned our latest expansion in the Middle East. We've been planning it for years, but the timing could hardly be worse, given the present political situation, and it's gone pear-shaped. I'm in trouble. So far I've kept it quiet, but I've got to do something about it quickly.'

Of course I knew all that. Research is one of the tools of my trade, though I don't usually spend time probing into the murky affairs of the City of London.

Giles sighed. 'Unless I can raise a decent amount of cash by the weekend, my business will collapse like a house of cards.'

'Surely things can't be that bad? Can't you sell off one of your subsidiaries, or close down a factory or two?'

'Too public, and too slow. Besides, it's not as simple to close down factories as it used to be. There's always hassle over redundancy payments for the workers . . . Oh, Tony, I'm sorry, that was tactless. Your father was made redundant, wasn't he? Just after we left school?'

'That's right. The firm he worked for was taken over by a larger company, who closed most of their UK factories and moved production to the Far East. Dad was the wrong side of fifty, and couldn't find another job. It broke his heart, and finally it killed him.'

'That's terrible. I was abroad by then, I didn't hear about it till later. If I'd known, I'd have got my father to offer him work.'

'I doubt it. It was your father who closed down his factory.'

He looked genuinely shocked. 'I'd no idea. Truly I hadn't . . . And you say it killed him? What happened?'

'Being unemployed was the final straw, coming after the publicity over Lisette's death. He hit the bottle in a big way, had a massive stroke, and died of it.'

Giles looked miserable, the picture of a kind, concerned friend. For a moment I remembered how close we had been. Would he really have helped me, if he'd known about Father?

But then he broke the spell. 'Perhaps now I can make it up to you. Just a little.'

'We'll see.' I put down my cup. 'Let's be clear. You want

me to help you sell this reproduction as a genuine first-century artefact.'

'Exactly. What do you say?'

The fish had taken the bait. 'I suppose it could work, if it was a private sale. But finding the right collector could be tricky. These things take time.'

'I've already found him. Norbert Van Lugenheyer, the New York millionaire. He collects ancient artefacts, he's as rich as Croesus, and he hates publicity.'

'Van Lugenheyer . . . that's quite a thought. He's prepared to pay a fortune for something he wants badly enough, and then he hoards all his treasures in his bank and never shows them to anybody. I have visions of him sitting and gloating over them at the dead of night. Yes, he might well fit the bill. What put you on to him?'

'It was Baker's idea, but I've checked, and he'd be perfect. But the approach would have to come from my agent. You, in other words. You know him, presumably?'

'Yes, in fact I've even advised him occasionally. He's got a wonderful Celtic collection. It's a pity he locks it away in a vault, I think beautiful things should be seen by as many people as possible. But for our purposes, it's an advantage.'

'"Our purposes". Does that mean you're with us?'

'Perhaps. I've one more question to ask.'

'What's in it for you?'

'That's the one.'

He rubbed his hands together. This kind of haggling was meat and drink to him. 'Baker wants twenty thousand in cash. I've agreed to that, it doesn't seem unreasonable, given that the boat will sell for seven figures. You and I will split the rest . . . say seventy-thirty?'

'You're joking, I hope.'

After a few minutes of enjoyable bargaining, we shook hands on fifty-fifty.

'I'll contact Van Lugenheyer this afternoon,' I said.

'As soon as you can, please. And remember, absolutely no publicity. I want my name kept right out of it.'

'Understood. You'll be "an anonymous vendor", I'll be your agent. Don't worry about a thing. Leave it all to me.'

'That's perfect. Thank you, Tony. Now, how about a spot of lunch to celebrate?'

But I had another appointment, and a more congenial companion to celebrate with.

Jack Baker's workshop is in the West End, tucked away behind the fashionable jewellery shop that sells most of his work. I never go there, because he likes to keep it as his private den where he can work away undisturbed. So we meet at a nearby pub, a small and rather scruffy place that we like because it hasn't been gentrified, and still welcomes ordinary working Londoners among the tourists and the posers.

I got there first and bought a pint for myself and a large glass of red wine for Jack. I took them to our usual corner table. As he walked in, I gave him a thumbs-up.

'It went well, Tony? Good. And you have bought something to celebrate with. Even better. To your health.' He sat down and took a long drink of wine.

'And yours. Yes, it went like clockwork, Jackie boy. I'm to ring Van Lugenheyer this afternoon. He'll help us, I'm sure of it. I'll get him to agree a nice juicy price.'

'This is not about money, Tony. Not for me, anyway.'

'Nor for me. But for Giles, that's exactly what it's about.'

You probably know the rest, it made quite a splash at the time. Of course some things never became public, such as the details of my phone conversations with Van Lugenheyer. I made other calls too, to journalists I knew, but only those I could trust not to be too discreet. Soon rumours began to circulate about the boat, its beauty, its probable value, and its possible sale to America. A few contacts rang me; I refused to comment, which fanned the flames of gossip nicely. It was as easy as burning down a forest by dropping a lighted cigarette end.

By evening, I was able to ring Giles and tell him Norbert had agreed a very satisfactory seven-figure sum. 'And he'll transfer the money between his bank and mine the minute the boat is in his hands. I'll take it over to New York myself. He's away from his office tomorrow, and can't take delivery till the day after. Is that OK?'

I could hear his smile over the phone. 'It's excellent. Well done, Tony. I'll get my people to book you a flight. Thanks again.'

By the next morning, the TV and radio news people had picked up the story and were running with it. An ancient and beautiful golden boat was being sold to an American collector – ought this to be allowed? – by an anonymous London vendor – who could it be? – for a fabulous price – just think of a number and add a few zeroes.

Shortly after noon Giles sent me a text. 'This is brilliant, Tony. Shakespeare had it wrong. All that glisters is gold this time.'

I texted back an obvious reply. 'Glad it's turning out as you like it.'

He didn't know that by then the forest fire had changed direction. More phone calls, a word here and a hint there, and out of nowhere came a suggestion that the boat wasn't, after all, a genuine Celtic artefact, followed by informed speculation about the names of the buyer and seller. Again, I gave no comment.

Giles rang me in a panic about eight. 'Tony, what's going on? The media seem to know about Van Lugenheyer, and a couple of reporters have even been on to me, wondering if I'm the anonymous vendor. I denied it, of course. But how did my name get out?'

'Don't worry. I expect they're ringing all sorts of people, just on the off-chance. Keep calm and hold your nerve. It'll all be over soon.'

'That's not the half of it. There's another rumour the boat isn't genuine first century.'

'I've heard that one too, but I'm not losing any sleep. The only people who know for sure are you, Baker and me. Remember, as long as we stand together, we won't fall apart.'

'But suppose Van Lugenheyer starts having second thoughts? Have you spoken to him today?'

'No. Tell you what, I'll ring him now and make sure he knows the score.'

It was a short conversation.

'Thanks for your help, Norbert, it's all going according to plan. I won't forget this.'

'Sure, Tony, no problem. Although I'm still not clear exactly what it is I'm helping with.'

'Just a bit of local politics, that's all.'

'So the less I know about it the better, right?'

'Right. Now it's time for the next stage.'

'You want me to announce publicly I've lost interest in the boat because I've heard disturbing rumours about its provenance.'

'That's it. And thanks again. I owe you a favour.'

'I'll hold you to that. If you ever get your hands on a real first-century golden boat, I expect to be the first to know, all right?'

'It's a deal.'

Next morning came the grim news that Giles' business empire had collapsed in a welter of huge debts and worthless shares. Giles and his wife had left London in their private jet, heading for South America. The gossipmongers revelled in speculation about their future. The serious commentators pontificated about the demise of yet another iconic British business. Nobody asked me anything at all.

When I got to our pub at midday, Jack was waiting, with champagne on ice.

'Well, Monsieur Boulanger,' I greeted him, 'we did it. It's finished.'

He got up, and we shook hands. 'I am glad. We have a kind of justice now. Of course it won't bring them back. But I am content.'

I nodded and filled our glasses. 'So am I. As the man said, all's well that ends well.'

'Ah no, we need no quotations today. Just a simple toast. To my sister, and your father. May they rest in peace.'

JUST TWO CLICKS
Peter James

Peter James, who currently chairs the Crime Writers' Association, is a film producer and scriptwriter whose series of detective novels featuring Roy Grace has been translated into more than thirty languages and has regularly featured in the bestseller lists.

J ust two clicks and Michael's face appeared. Margaret pressed her fingers against the screen, in a longing to stroke his slender, Pre-Raphaelite face and to touch that long, wavy hair that lay tantalizingly beyond the glass.

Joe was downstairs watching a football match on Sky. What she was doing was naughty. Wicked temptation! But didn't Socrates say the unexamined life is not worth living? The kids were gone. Empty nesters now, just herself and Joe. Joe was like a rock to which her life was moored. Safe, strong, but dull. And right now she didn't want a rock, she wanted a knight on a white charger. The knight who was just two clicks away.

Just two clicks and Margaret's face would be in front of him! Michael's fingers danced lightly across the keys of his laptop, caressing them sensually.

They had been emailing each other for over a year – in fact, as Margaret had reminded Michael this afternoon, for exactly one year, two months, three days and nineteen hours!

And now, tomorrow evening, at half past seven, in just over twenty-two hours' time, they were finally going to meet. Their first *real* date.

Both of them had had a few obstacles to deal with first. Like Margaret's husband, Joe. During the course of a thousand increasingly passionate emails (actually, one thousand, one hundred and eighty-seven, as Margaret had informed him this afternoon), Michael had built up a mental picture of Joe: a tall, mean, no-brainer of a bully who had once punched a front door down with his bare fists. He'd built up a mental picture of Margaret, also, that was far more elaborate than the single photograph he had downloaded so long ago of a pretty redhead, who looked a little like Scully from the *X-Files*. In fact, quite a lot like the heavenly Scully.

'We shouldn't really meet, should we?' she had emailed him this afternoon. 'It might spoil everything between us!'

Michael's wife, Karen, had walked out on him two months ago, blaming the time he spent on the internet, telling him he was more in love with his computer than her.

Well, actually sweetheart, with someone on my computer, he had nearly said, but hadn't quite plucked up the courage. That had always been his problem. Lack of courage. And of course, right now this was fuelled by an image of Joe, who could punch a front door down with his bare fists.

A new email from Margaret lay in his inbox. 'Twenty-two hours and seven minutes! I'm so excited, I can't wait to meet you, my darling. Have you decided where? M xxxxx'

'Me neither!' he typed. 'Do you know the Red Lion in Handcross? It has deep booths, very discreet. Went to a Real Ale tasting there recently. Midway between us. I don't know how I'm going to sleep tonight! All my love. Michael xxxx'

Margaret opened the email eagerly, and then, as she read it, for the first time in one year, two months and three days she felt the presence of clouds in her heart. *Real Ale?* He'd never mentioned an interest in Real Ale before. Real Ale was a bit of an anoraks' thing, wasn't it? *Midway between us?* Did he mean he couldn't be bothered to drive to somewhere close to her? But, worst of all . . .

A pub???

She typed her reply. 'I don't do pubs, my darling. I do weekends in Paris at the George V, or maybe the Ritz Carlton or the Bristol.'

Then she deleted it. I'm being stupid, dreaming, all shot to hell by my nerves . . . From downstairs there was a 'Whoop!'

from Joe, and then she could hear tumultuous roaring. A goal. Great. Big deal. Wow, Joe, I'm so happy for you.

Deleting her words, she replaced them with: 'Darling, the Red Lion sounds wickedly romantic. 7.30. I'm not going to sleep either! All my love. M xxxx'

What if Joe had been reading her emails and was going to tail her tonight to the Red Lion? Michael thought, pulling up in the farthest, darkest corner of the car park. He climbed out of his pea-green Astra (Karen had taken the BMW) and walked nervously towards the front entrance of the pub, freshly showered and shaven, his breath minted, his body marinated in a Boss cologne Karen had once said made him smell manly, his belly feeling like it was filled with deranged moths.

He stopped just outside and checked his macho diver's watch. 7.32. Taking a deep breath he went in.

And saw her right away.

Oh no.

His heart did not so much sink as burrow its way down to the bottom of his brand new Docksider yachting loafers.

She was sitting at the bar, in full public display – OK, the place was pretty empty – but worse than that, a packet of cigarettes and a lighter lay on the counter in front of her. She'd never told him that she smoked. But far, far, far worst of all, the bitch looked nothing like the photograph she had sent him. Nothing at all!

True it was the same red hair colour – well, henna-dyed red, at any rate – but there were no long tresses to caress – it had been cropped short and gelled into spikes that looked sharp enough to prick your fingers on. *You never told me you'd cut your hair. Why not???* Her face was plain, and she was a good three or four stone heavier than in the photograph, with cellulite-pocked thighs bared by a vulgar skirt. She hadn't lied about her age, but that was just about the only thing. And she'd caught his eye and was now smiling at him.

No. Absolutely not. No which way. Sorry. Sorry. Sorry.

Michael turned, without looking back, and fled.

Roaring out of the parking lot, haemorrhaging perspiration in anger and embarrassment, switching off his mobile phone in case she tried to ring, he had to swerve to avoid some idiot driving in far too fast.

'Dickhead!' he shouted.

Margaret was relieved to see the car park was almost empty. Pulling into the farthest corner, she turned on the interior light, checked her face and her hair in the mirror, then climbed out and locked the car. 7.37. Just late enough, hopefully, for Michael to have arrived first. Despite her nerves, she walked on air through the front entrance.

To her disappointment there was no sign of him. A couple of young salesmen types at a table. A solitary elderly man. And on the bar stools, a plump, middle-aged woman with spiky red hair and a tarty skirt, who was joined by a tattooed, denim-clad gorilla who emerged from the gents, nuzzled her neck greedily, making her giggle, then retrieved a smouldering cigarette from the ashtray.

Michael, in his den, stared at the screen. 'Bitch,' he said. 'What a bitch!' With one click he dragged all Margaret's emails to his trash bin. With another, he dragged her photograph to the same place. Then he emptied the trash.

Back home just before ten, Joe glanced up from a football game that looked like all the other football games Margaret had ever seen. 'What happened to your night out with the girls?' he asked.

'I decided I'd been neglecting my husband too much recently.' She put her arm around him, around her rock and kissed his cheek. 'I love you,' she said.

He actually took his eyes off the game to look at her, and then kissed her back. 'I love you, too,' he said.

Then she went upstairs to her room, and checked her mailbox. There was nothing. 'Michael, I waited two hours,' she began typing.

Then she stopped. It was cold in her den. Downstairs the television had given a cosy glow. And her rock had felt warm.

Sod you, Michael.

Just two clicks and he was gone from her life.

The Visitor

H.R.F. Keating

H. R. F. Keating, a former chair of the Crime Writers' Association and President of the Detection Club, twice won the CWA Gold Dagger and also received the CWA Cartier Diamond Dagger. A prolific novelist and short story writer, he was also a prominent critic of, and commentator on, the crime genre. He died in 2011. It is believed that this story, featuring the renowned Inspector Ghote, has only previously appeared in a Penguin India collection published in the 1990s.

Paperwork, Inspector Ghote thought. Sitting here at my desk signing this, signing that. Routine also. Each and every crime seeming in the end just only the same. In detective books all is excitement, hundred per cent baffling mysteries, utmost shocking revelations. And in Bombay Crime Branch, what it is? Paperwork, paperwork, paperwork. Plus also routines. Routines, routines, rout . . .

A shadow fell over the sprawl of papers in front of him.

He looked up, realizing that absorbed in his thoughts he had heard only subconsciously the batwing doors open and clap to again. He saw now, standing looming over his desk, a big broad-shouldered Westerner. A fair-haired young man, perhaps not quite thirty, wearing a light-coloured suit, an open-necked shirt.

And what is this? A white man truly white. Paper-white. Blood-drained white.

Suddenly he thought that if he himself had been born only some twenty years earlier, seeing a white man shocked out of his senses, as this fellow standing in front of his desk clearly was – he was even unsteadily swaying a little – he would have felt as if he was confronting a sight he ought never to have witnessed. Some god revealed as a figure of straw. A maharani caught in a state of nakedness.

But this was now. Not that distant time.

'Sit, sit,' he said to the young man. 'You are feeling faint, yes?'

'Yes. I . . . Yes. Thanks . . . Is it Inspector . . . er . . . Inspector Ghote? They told me . . .'

The swaying youngster – he had a British accent – managed to pull back one of the chairs lined up in front of the desk. He slid down on to it, but could do no more afterwards than to put his head in his hands.

Ghote allowed him time to recover.

'Yes?' he said at last. 'They were directing you to my cabin?'

'Yes. Yes. But yes, I'm sorry, I did feel faint. You were quite right. You see, I've just had a shock. I – I hoped it wasn't. But it is. And it's a shock. A terrible shock.'

Once more he fell silent and Ghote let him sit there.

'Now, what sort of a shock is it?' he enquired eventually.

'I've just – I've just learnt. No. No. I'd better tell you the whole thing. As it happened.'

But having said that much, the young man fell yet again into a deep reverie.

At last Ghote prompted him, a little sharply. 'Perhaps it would be best if you are giving full particulars. Name, place of residence, date of birth, occupation?'

'Yes, yes. You'll need to know all that. In the end. So, yes. Right. Henry Reymond. Er – from Britain. Residence, was it you asked? Yes, it's 35 Northumberland Place, London, W2. Date of birth: October 31, 1966. Occupation – I'm in the travel business. I work for a London firm called Experience India. But I haven't been with them long, and this – this is the first time I've been here. To India. Yes. You see, they sent me to Calcutta. To explore the possibilities of Calcutta as a tourist centre.'

'But you are here in Bombay itself.'

'Yes, yes. I had to come. To check. Yes. To check whether . . . And – and I found that it was true. All true.'

'Mr Reymond, I am thinking you are once more becoming altogether confused. Kindly begin from the beginning and proceed to final end.'

'Yes, you're right, Inspector. That'll be the only way you'll ever come to understand.'

'Very well, what is this beginning?'

'Oh yes, I know what that was. It was when I had just arrived at Calcutta airport. Virtually in my first few minutes on Indian soil. I did say I had never been here before, didn't I?'

'Yes, yes. You were telling so.'

'Yes. My first time here. And I've only been working for Experience India for a few months. Before that I was with a firm in England that specializes in holidays in Spain. So I actually know almost nothing about India. But someone fell ill, and my boss thought I could probably manage this exploratory trip in his place. He – he said it might even be an advantage, me knowing nothing about India. I'd sort of see things the way our future customers would . . . But – but I'm losing track again. No, you see, it was while I was in the car our Delhi representative had arranged for me, going from Dum Dum airport to the hotel, that it all began to happen.'

Henry Reymond licked at his dry lips. 'I'd exchanged a few words with the driver. He'd asked if this was my first visit, and I'd said it was. His English was OK but a bit difficult to understand. So after that – I was terribly tired after the flight – I just sat there looking out at what I could see in the dark, not thinking of anything much. And then – it was just after we'd got into the city itself, then I . . .'

Henry Reymond came to a complete check. Total silence.

'And then, Mr Reymond?'

'Then? What . . .? Oh yes, I was telling you. Well, then . . . then all of a sudden I leant forward and I said something.'

'Yes? What it was? It is somehow important, no?'

'Important? Yes. Yes, it bloody well is. You see, I said something, but I did not at all know what it was. Words had come out of my mouth. But I didn't know what they meant. They were sort of – well, mellifluous words, but I had no idea what I was saying. But then my driver just turned his head back towards me and answered. In the same sort of gentle rounded language. And I realized then that the words I had spoken had been asking if the monsoon floods were still there.'

Henry Reymond looked at Ghote almost beseechingly.

'Inspector,' he said, 'believe me. I had spoken in a language

I didn't at all know. I know what it was now. It was Bengali. But Inspector, I don't know any Bengali. I'd never to my knowledge heard a word of it spoken. I don't speak any of the Indian languages. Not a word. In the firm they told me anyone I'd have any dealings with would speak English.'

'And this is what is causing you so much troubles?' Ghote asked. 'I am thinking: no problem.'

'Oh, if it was only that, just seeming to speak Bengali. Or actually speaking it. I hardly thought about it at the time there in the car. I suppose I was too sort of stunned to say anything more. And then we arrived at the hotel, the Oberoi Grand, and as soon as I'd got to my room I simply collapsed on the bed and fell asleep.'

'So perhaps this was some dream you were having, and not at all what had actually happened.'

'Well, that's what I thought in the morning. I convinced myself of it. But that wasn't all.'

'Something more was happening?'

'Yes, it was. Quite a simple thing really. But – well, it made me realize I couldn't have dreamt it all, about speaking Bengali.'

'So what it was?'

'Just this. After I'd had breakfast I thought I'd just take a stroll outside, to sort of get the feel of the place. Of Calcutta.'

'And . . .?'

'And almost at once I came across a stall selling sweets. In the arcade there, in the street, the street called Chowringhee. And – and I knew straight off what the sweets in one of the heaps in the stall were called. *Sandesh*. And I knew that I liked *sandesh*. Very, very much. But Inspector, till that moment I'd never heard the word, I swear. I mean, there are places in England where there are lots of Indians, and I think the shops sell Indian sweets. But I've never been near any of them. And yet I knew I liked *sandesh*. I bought some at once and knew that, though they were sort of gluey, they would easily break in half and that my fingers would get sugary as I did that. I knew, too, just how they would taste. Of boiled-down curdled milk. And when I ate the first one I even knew it was not quite the best kind. It was not *karraa pakar*. But Inspector, how could

I have known those exact words, those Bengali words? And how could I have known what was the best kind of *sandesh*?'

Ghote wondered how he could explain it in a way that would calm this almost hysterical young Englishman. But before he had arrived at any conclusion Henry Reymond burst out again.

'Inspector, it means that in another life I was a Bengali. Doesn't it? I was a Bengali. Me. Me. It means that, doesn't it? It must.'

'Well, yes, that would be so. But Mr Reymond it is not something of too much dismay.'

'Oh, I know what you are thinking. And yes, I could have come to terms with it. If that was all. An Indian in a former life. It'd be something to talk about back home, joke about even.'

'But it is not all?'

'God, no. It's not. It's not. You see almost at once I got an inkling of the full horror of it all. Eating my *sandesh* and sort of pondering the extraordinary fact of me knowing what it was, I walked on and turned into a road I knew, without having to look for any street sign, was called Park Street. I knew that. Knew it. And I knew that it led to the Park Street Cemetery. That must have been the former-life Bengali inside me, telling me that. But me, there in the present, I remembered, too, that my boss in London had told me that the Park Street Cemetery, with all its tombs of Britons of the past, could be one of the sights to put in this planned tour of ours. So I went inside, I wandered about. I'd almost forgotten that Bengali business. And then, suddenly . . .'

In an instant then, the young Briton lost all the faint returning colour that had come into his cheeks.

Tea, Ghote thought.

He reached across his desk for the bell to call a peon. But before he had banged down the bell's knob the young man spoke again.

'Inspector . . .' The word came almost crawling out from between suddenly parched lips. 'Inspector, there in the cemetery I saw the place where I had left the body. On the tomb of Colonel William Kirkpatrick. Inspector, I committed murder.'

'You have been committing murder? In the Park Street Cemetery in Calcutta itself? When were you doing such? And why also? And why have you come to Bombay to confess? If it is confession you are giving.'

'I came here – I had to come here to make absolutely sure. That's why. You see, it was from Bombay that I went to Calcutta in the first place. Or that Pranav Bandopadhyaya, lecturer in Bengali at Bombay University, went back on impulse to Calcutta that day in 1937. I – or he. Or me. I don't know. But I know that about a year before I had taken it into my head to send a Diwali card to – to the girl I was once in love with, Rekha. Rekha, who had been hurriedly married to that rich swine when her parents found out about us. And months later a letter had come from her, telling me she had long ago left the swine, had lived a miserable, hand-to-mouth life and, I gathered between her lines, was now the mistress of a Scotsman in a big Calcutta shipping firm, who was abominably ill-treating her, locking her inside when he chose to go away, forcing her to obey him in everything. And that letter happened to arrive the very day university classes finished. So, without a word to anyone, I rushed out, jumped into a Victoria, went to V.T. Station and caught the Calcutta mail.'

For a moment Ghote wanted to ask why, if there was so much hurry, he had not taken a plane. Then he realized. 1937. The man sitting in front of him in Bombay Police Headquarters in the year 1996 was talking about going to Calcutta in 1937.

'So after two days I was reaching, late in the night, to the Howrah station.' Was the English now coming from the mouth of the young man acquiring a Bengali lilt? 'There I was at once taking a rickshaw, with just only enough sense to go so far as Sealdah station. From there I would walk to the flat where the Scotsman was keeping Rekha. It was the night of Purnima, a full moon. But there was no one to see me, except more rickshaw wallahs sleeping by the roadsides. As I hurried onwards all I was hearing was the ting-ting of their bells as I passed.'

Could this fellow have truly been there? Ghote asked himself. Certainly what he was telling was altogether vivid.

And yet Mr Henry Reymond had, if he was to be believed, never been to India in his life.

'So at last I reached the address Rekha had put on her letter. The door of the place was standing wide open. I am not knowing why. Perhaps the Scotsman had only just come himself and had carelessly left it. And then, from above, I was hearing Rekha's voice. Crying out. Begging for mercy only. So I was creeping upwards, quickly but carefully also. Luckily an iron staircase was there, so I was making no noise. And then . . .'

Henry Reymond – or was it Pranav Bandopadhyaya? – took in a great noisy gulp of air.

'He was standing over her, Inspector,' he whispered. 'He had a horsewhip. At once I flung myself at him. I sent him to the ground, but I fell also with him. And in an instant he had rolled over and his great red hands were round my throat. I thought my final moment had come. But in my agonies my arms were threshing to and fro on the floor and one of my hands touched some metal object. I grasped it. It was heavy, curved and very, very sharp. What they call in Bombay a *chhura*.'

'A chopper,' Ghote heard himself murmur in English.

But Henry Reymond, no, Pranav Bandopadhyaya who was speaking, no doubt about that, simply went on with his account of what had happened in those distant days of the British Raj.

'Rekha told me afterwards she had been chopping spices, and the chopper had fallen to the ground when the Scotsman had come in and seized hold of her.'

Once more Henry Reymond paused, gasped for air.

'I killed him then,' he said. 'I brought that thing down on the back of his neck with my utmost force. It was almost cutting off his head.'

'You are hundred per cent certain of all this?' Ghote said at last, speaking into the deep silence.

'Yes, yes. But the thing was, Rekha was wonderful.' And now had the English voice taken over once more? 'Without Rekha I would have just lain there in that man's blood and waited for something, for anything, to happen. But Rekha saw at once how to get rid of the body. The house looked over the

wall of the Park Street Cemetery. She made me heave that
heavy, red-faced corpse out, and in the moonlight I saw the
name on the tomb where it fell. *Sacred to the Memory of
Colonel William Kirkpatrick.* Then, when Rekha found no one
knew I had come to Calcutta, she cleaned me up and simply
sent me straight back to Bombay. The Scotsman's death, she
promised me, would be put down to dacoits hiding in the
cemetery. I wanted her to come to Bombay with me, but
she refused. She said it would only make me more conspicuous.
And – and I never heard from her again. I wrote within a week
to that flat she had been installed in, taking care not to use
my name at all. But the letter was returned marked "*Not
known*". So I never went back to Calcutta, never.'

Ghote saw that sweat had begun again to spring up on the
pale face in front of him.

'Look,' Henry Reymond said, leaning earnestly forward,
'when it came into my head, there in Calcutta, in the Park
Street Cemetery, that I might have somehow in my former life
committed murder, I thought – I'm really quite level-headed
you know – that the thing I had to do before anything else
was to find out if such a murder had really occurred. Well,
that morning at breakfast in the hotel I had been reading *The
Statesman*, and I remembered seeing that the paper had been
going strong as far back as the 1930s. So I went round there
and asked if I could possibly see the files. Very decently they
took them out for me. And I confirmed then that a certain
James McFarlane, a shipping company manager, had been
found brutally murdered, the report said, in the Park Street
Cemetery. Then I looked through the files for a good many
weeks onwards, but I saw no report of anyone being appre-
hended for the crime.'

Ghote felt now that he was beginning to see what had
brought the young Englishman hurry-scurrying to Bombay.
He must need to know whether such a person as the Bengali
he thought he had been had ever existed.

'And now,' he said slowly and carefully, 'you have found
out that one Pranav Bandopadhyaya was here in Bombay itself
in the year 1937.'

'Yes, you're right, Inspector. You see, even when I had

discovered that in some mysterious way there had come into my head facts about a murder in the past that no one else, apparently, had ever known about, I still wanted proof that I was that Pranav Bandopadhyaya who had committed the murder. So I took the first flight here that I could get, and, yes, Bombay University records show that one Pranav Bandopadhyaya was a lecturer in Bengali here in 1937. He had eventually retired and received a pension until the date of his death, October 31, 1966. And you know what date that is, don't you?'

For an instant it eluded Ghote. Then he knew. *Date of birth: October the thirty-first 1966.* The young man in front of him had said just that when, attempting to get him into a rational state of mind, he had asked him in his best official manner to provide his bio-data. 31 October, the day of the death of the Bengali who, in 1937, had, or had not, murdered a certain Scotsman.

'Day of your birth itself,' he said.

The young English visitor almost rose out of his chair. 'Inspector,' he said, voice creaking with suppressed fears, 'I killed James McFarlane. I did. I did. It was me. I've come to you to confess to it. So, please, Inspector, what are you going to do?'

Tears were standing in the young Englishman's eyes.

Inspector Ghote permitted himself a small smile.

'Mr Henry Reymond,' he said. 'You are citizen of UK only, a visitor to our India of 1996, a nation that has been independent almost to fifty years. Very well, you have, so to say it, had as a visitor inside yourself, some Bengali fellow from days of British Raj now long dead and forgotten also. Perhaps it is only in India, with our so many millions of people, that such things are found quite often to occur, even although the science of the West would not like to acknowledge same. But occur they do. They are just only something that is happening in life. Mr Reymond, kindly visit the India of reality.

THE CASE OF
THE VANISHING VAGRANT

An Inspector Faro Mystery

Alanna Knight

Alanna Knight is a novelist, biographer and playwright. Author of more than forty books, she is an expert on Scottish history and an authority on Robert Louis Stevenson. Her crime fiction includes the Inspector Faro mysteries, set in Victorian Edinburgh.

Edinburgh, 1882

'That's where it happened, Faro.' Dr Winton indicated the house opposite. 'Eight years ago and they never got anyone. That was the summer you were at Balmoral. Rumours of an assassination attempt, weren't there?'

'More than rumours,' Inspector Jeremy Faro, Her Majesty's personal detective, said grimly, and it had cut short his time with his two motherless daughters on holiday from Orkney with their grandmother.

Across the street, a mirror image of the doctor's own highly respectable middle-class semi-villa, the murder house with a For Sale notice in its overgrown garden looked too mild for violence.

Dealing out the playing cards, the police doctor continued, 'Apparently it was some old vagrant, wandered down the side of the house, broke the kitchen window, crept upstairs, smothered Fanshaw where he slept. And disappeared again. Remarkable.'

'Remarkable indeed. That no one heard him. Surely that broken glass made enough noise?'

'Indeed. Woke Mrs Dora Fanshaw and Mrs Wade, the

housekeeper. But Fanshaw rarely went to bed sober, so they presumed that he'd knocked over a glass of water.'

'Any clues?'

'None. No apparent motive either. Police absolutely baffled. Only possible verdict: murder by person or persons unknown.'

From Faro's vast experience murder had to have a motive. 'The most likely reason would have been that Fanshaw tackled an intruder.'

Winton shook his head. 'I was called in. No evidence of a struggle, nothing disturbed or stolen. In their evidence, Mrs Dora – his cousin by marriage – said that she and Mrs Wade made a thorough search. Not even a silver spoon missing. That was odd with valuables for the picking, including Fanshaw's timepiece and wallet on his bedside table.'

'So we are left with the only other logical conclusion. That the victim was known to the killer. A known enemy with a score to settle, a close friend or member of the family. Indeed, it is not unknown for the murderer to be revealed as the person who first discovers the body.'

Pausing to shed a tenative ace, Faro sat back. 'A passing vagrant does not fit any of these categories.'

'My game, Faro!' said Winton triumphantly, scooping up the handful of coins. 'Never mind, old chap,' he added heartily. 'As they say, unlucky at cards, lucky in love.'

Faro smiled sadly. 'In my case, alas, neither.'

Considering the inspector's still youthful appearance, his thick fair hair and excellent bone structure – the ultimate Viking inheritance of the Orkney Isles – Winton decided that his friend was being exceptionally modest.

'You weren't paying enough attention to the game,' he added kindly. 'You threw away that trick. Perhaps your mind was elsewhere.'

Faro nodded absently. Later, as he was leaving, he suggested a closer look at the murder house. 'Come with me, Winton, you can tell the neighbours that I am a would-be buyer.'

Dr Winton thought that unlikely, but led the way, pushing open the gate leading past the kitchen door to an enclosed walled garden, with a door into the back lane for tradesmen's deliveries and access to the coal cellar.

The Fanshaw grocery chain provided the splendid chutney to accompany Faro's breakfast sausage and bacon. The founder Thomas Fanshaw was responsible for the marmalade, made from his grandmother's recipe in a dingy tenement kitchen to sell on market day stalls. A story of rags to riches.

Sadly, Thomas lost his first wife in childbirth and remarried late in life, an attractive young lady called Dora Wills, first brought to his attention in an amateur production of 'School for Scandal'. He was delighted to encounter her off-stage serving behind the counter in a Fanshaw shop.

Marriage swiftly followed but alas, Thomas did not long survive and left Dora a grieving childless widow to discover that the business passed to Ronald Fanshaw – a very different individual to his kindly older cousin.

Few things kept Faro from a good night's sleep, apart from toothache and an unsolved mystery; the latter decided him, that although the trail had long since gone cold he would not be satisfied until he had carefully re-examined all the evidence in this baffling case.

At the Central Office of the Edinburgh City Police, enquiries for the file revealed that his newly acquired Sergeant Brodie had not only been involved as a witness but that the house-keeper was related to his wife.

'Mrs Wade,' said Brodie, 'a widow, only son a deep-sea sailor. Loyal family retainer, devoted to Mrs Dora. No serv-ants, a daily maid and Duncan the gardener who was short on temper and stone deaf.'

'Any visitors or guests at the time of the murder?' Faro asked.

'Only decorators from a Glasgow firm. But they went back home on the train every night.'

'What exactly were they decorating?'

'Fanshaw had taken over the master bedroom from Mrs Dora. A mean man, pretty heartless, everyone agreed. Best room in the house, moved everything of value with him, including a very valuable new Aubusson carpet from the drawing room.'

Faro had been making notes of his own. 'Excellent, Brodie. Now, if you will be so good as to leave the file with me.'

'I can do better than that, sir,' the sergeant said with a grin. 'I was one of the few people who actually met the murderer,' he added triumphantly. 'The Fanshaw residence was on my regular daily beat in Minto Place. Until the murder, nothing exciting ever happened, apart from rescuing lost dogs and cats up trees—'

'And the murderer?' Faro interrupted.

'Ah yes. One day I observed a shabby old vagrant. Long ragged coat, battered hat pulled well down, muffled up to the eyes. Loitering about in what could only be called a suspicious manner. So I called out, polite as you like, "Good afternoon, sir. Can I help you?" Well, one look at my uniform and he was off. Very fleet too, for an old chap.' He shook his head. 'Felt a bit sorry for him, guessed that he'd fallen on bad times.'

'What made you think that, Sergeant?'

'His boots, Inspector. As he ran I noticed his boots, very spruce, in far better shape than the rest of his apparel.'

'Remarkably observant, Sergeant! Pray continue.'

Brodie grinned. 'Thank you, sir. Well, dashing off like that confirmed he was up to no good. So I set off after him. The garden gate of the Fanshaw residence was open. He rushed in, slammed it shut. By the time I got it unlatched, he'd disappeared across the lawn. The back lane door was bolted, so he must have leapt the wall. Duncan was in his greenhouse; I shouted but he just stared at me, deaf as I told you.

'Suddenly Mrs Fanshaw appeared. She'd seen it all from the kitchen window. Told me to wait while she went for Mrs Wade who had taken Mr Fanshaw his afternoon tea upstairs. Terrified she was, some wild story that this was the same man who'd been sending her vile letters.' Brodie shook his head. 'Didn't quite fit the old beggar I'd just seen.'

'The condition of the tramp's boots might well indicate an educated man,' Faro said as the sergeant pointed to the file.

'Both the ladies' statements are here, sir.'

Reading them, Faro was particularly interested in Mrs Dora's account of the incident at the enquiry.

'I was preparing a meal and when I saw this vagrant enter the garden I knew I was in terrible danger. He had been lurking about outside the house and sending notes threatening to kill me.'

Questioned as to the postmark on these notes, Mrs Fanshaw had said, 'There was none. They had been pushed through the letter box. But I was sure the sender was Ronald, especially as the words were composed of capital letters cut from his daily newspaper and stuck on the same brand of notepaper that he used.'

Asked why he should send her notes, she replied, 'My late cousin-in-law was a practical joker of the vilest nature. He enjoyed scaring people, especially any children in the street. Even as a child I learned that he was cruel to small animals. I thought this was just one of his crude efforts to persuade me to marry him. I was not deceived that he loved me. What he really wanted were my shares of the Fanshaw business.'

Asked how many of these notes she had received, Mrs Dora said firmly, 'Four in four weeks. The first three said, "Ask not for whom the bell tolls. Take care, Dora Fanshaw". I recognized the quotation from John Donne, a favourite of Ronald's. In his less aggressive moments he was fond of quoting poetry.

'The last one the week he died was the worst. It said, "The bell tolls for thee, Dora Fanshaw. You are a dead woman". I confronted him but he just laughed. Said he had more to do than write silly notes to scare silly women. Again he insisted that I marry him then I need fear no one.'

The final question was, why she had not informed the police? She responded that Mrs Wade urged her to do so. But afraid that Ronald would throw her out of the house if she involved the police or tried to damage his reputation, she threw them on the fire.

Faro turned to Mrs Wade's statement which added no new material, beyond the fact that the notes might have provided vital evidence concerning the killer's identity.

At his meeting with Sergeant Brodie the following day Faro had made some observations of his own.

'Considering Fanshaw as a practical joker trying to frighten

Mrs Dora into marrying him, one might well imagine the sinister vagrant as Fanshaw himself.'

Brodie nodded eagerly. 'And that would account for his good boots, except that when I was pursuing him, Mrs Wade was taking him his tea upstairs. He couldn't have been in two places at once, could he now?'

'Nor could he have committed suicide by smothering himself with a pillow, Sergeant.'

Brodie shook his head. 'That just isn't logical, sir.'

'There is a lot that isn't logical about this case,' Faro said grimly to his sergeant.

He turned again to Mrs Dora's statement. 'I awoke in the middle the night to the sound of breaking glass. It was still dark. I told myself it came from the master bedroom opposite and that Ronald had dropped his glass tumbler. I fell asleep again and was downstairs first, usually it is Mrs Wade and although she is in poor health she refuses to abandon her duties.

'When I saw the glass on the back door window had been broken – and the bolt was undone, I was terrified. Mrs Wade rushed downstairs and cried, "Something terrible has happened, madam: I think Mr Ronald is dead".'

Faro then turned to Mrs Wade's statement. 'I have a rigid daily routine each morning. Mr Ronald insisted that I awaken him and bring fresh towels and linen before making his morning tea. I noticed that the door to the master bedroom was ajar. I tapped on it and, receiving no response, I went in quietly and opened the shutters. I saw that he was sleeping on his back with a pillow over his head. This seemed odd so I went to wake him up. His ghastly countenance told me he was dead. He had been smothered.

'I went downstairs to Mrs Dora, and she began to scream, pointing to shattered glass. The sound had awakened her during the night. Oddly enough it had awakened me in my room at the end of the corridor, but we had both assumed that Mr Ronald had knocked the glass off his bedside table on his way to the WC. I just took one of my doctor's pills and went back to sleep. We both realized there had been a break-in during the night and that the burglar had murdered Mr Ronald.

'PC Brodie was going past on his early morning beat. I told him Mr Ronald had had a terrible accident.'

Laying aside the file, Faro said to Brodie, 'When you followed Mrs Wade into the house, what did you observe?'

'I remember trying to avoid broken glass all over the path. In the kitchen, Mrs Fanshaw still sobbing. Upstairs with Mrs Wade. One look and I knew the gentleman was dead. Downstairs again, Mrs Wade made us both a cup of tea while I took down her statement about the noise the intruder had made that had awakened them. Then I went into the garden, in case there were any clues.'

Faro said, 'Describe exactly what you saw, if you please.'

Brodie frowned in concentration. 'Nothing but fragments of glass from the broken window.'

'Any footprints?'

'First thing I looked for, sir. We were having a dry spell. Ground was hard as a bone. Duncan was furious about having to clear the broken glass, accused me of stamping all over his flower beds. That was my last worry, with a dead man upstairs.'

'How did he take that?'

'Pretty cool, I thought. Said nothing just shrugged. I got the impression he was not particularly fond of his employer either. On my way out back to the station, I told Dr Winton and the ladies not to touch anything upstairs until the police detectives arrived.'

Later that week, Faro went to visit the doctor again.

Seated at the window, the empty house, scene of an unsolved murder that now intrigued him, looked gloomier than ever.

Faro sighed. 'If only walls – and a garden – could talk, Winton.'

Winton laughed. 'It is really haunting you! I'm disappointed, I thought you would have solved it by now,' he added slyly.

Faro shook his head. 'There are so many baffling elements. I believe I have sorted some of them. Had Fanshaw any enemies among the neighbours?'

'Hardly a popular man. But there is a great deal of difference between personal dislike and committing murder.'

'Exactly so, Doctor. So the only logical motive remains – who was to gain by Fanshaw's death; who was to inherit?

'Everything went to Mrs Dora since Ronald Fanshaw, although once married, had no heirs, his wife had divorced him some years earlier.'

'Ah, and the whereabouts of this ex-wife?'

'Remarried, proved to be living in America at the time of his death.'

'Business rivals?'

'Mrs Dora had always kept in close touch with the Fanshaw shops. Shares and contacts, she would have heard of any business rivals. A difficult man but no indications that he had ever been threatened with physical abuse. As for Mrs Dora, she was aware that Fanshaw was going bankrupt thanks to his faulty speculations. She had naught to gain but the prospect of moving into a less expensive house.'

Pausing, Winton thought for a moment. 'You have insisted that there has to be a motive, and certainly this particular murder makes no sense without it. There is another strand to this mystery and it may indeed be the key to solving it. By opening the door to yet another murder – a failed one this time.'

'Indeed! And that was?' Faro demanded eagerly.

Winton placed his fingertips together. 'Mrs Dora believed that it was herself who was the intended victim.'

At Faro's astonished expression, he smiled indulgently. 'Consider for a moment that Ronald was murdered in the marital bed Mrs Dora had once shared with her late husband.'

And Faro remembered the story of the switched bedrooms and Winton continued: 'The intruder knew the exact layout of the house, the way to the master bedroom. Shutters closed, in the curtained bed, just a head on the pillow. Someone who knew the house during the late Mr Thomas Fanshaw's occupancy but was unaware of the changes. A case of mistaken identity.'

Faro thought for a moment. 'Well, that eliminates the two Glasgow decorators. What about the gardener, Duncan? Surely he would have a fair idea of what the interior of the house looked like.'

Winton smiled dryly. 'Our gardeners know their place. Never a muddy boot further than the kitchen door, he wouldn't have the faintest idea of where any of them slept.'

Faro remembered Duncan's brief statement that he had seen a tramp wandering about a couple of times and told him to clear off. Described him as: 'Shabby clothes. Looked a bit simple, like.'

'What about Mrs Wade's sailor son?' he asked Winton.

'He couldn't possibly be the vagrant, Faro, seen several times prior to the murder while he was on the high seas. That night his ship was in dry-dock at Greenock. As first mate he was on duty. It's all on record.'

Faro's feeling that the doctor knew a great deal more than he was prepared to admit was confirmed next morning when discussing the case with Brodie.

The sergeant sighed deeply. 'Now that so many of the people have gone, sir, I can let you into a family secret concerning Mrs Wade, a skeleton in the cupboard, so to speak.

'After she died shortly after Fanshaw, my wife Nell said it was common knowledge in the family that Peter Wade was in fact Thomas Fanshaw's natural son whom he refused to recognize.'

'Now that is interesting. Was Mrs Dora aware of this relationship?'

Brodie grinned broadly. 'I expect so, Inspector, seeing that she married him the following year. They emigrated to Australia. Nell – my wife – got cards from them at Christmas until Dora died a couple of years ago. Sad, nice family with a couple of youngsters. Peter went back to sea and didn't keep in touch.'

'And for us, Sergeant, the loss of one promising supect, an illegitimate son with a very strong motive for resenting Ronald Fanshaw.'

'You have some ideas of your own, sir?'

'I have indeed, although our main suspect is still the vagrant, whom you yourself gave chase to on one occasion.'

Faro was seized by a fit of coughing. Brodie brought him a glass of water and after drinking deeply, he replaced it on the table and referred to his notes. 'You commented on the vagrant's shabby clothes. You even observed his excellent footwear.'

'True, sir. But none of us ever got a close look at him. He was always muffled up. Very sharp about that.'

Faro smiled broadly. 'But you, Sergeant, are to be congratulated in providing the one vital clue to his identity.'

'I am?' Brodie looked bewildered.

'Let us go back to when Fanshaw's killer entered by the kitchen door after breaking the window. Confirmed by both Mrs Fanshaw and Mrs Wade who heard the sound but presumed Ronald Fanshaw had upset a glass, like this one. Am I right?'

Brodie nodded and Faro went on: 'So if you will now observe this carefully, Sergeant.'

So saying, Faro dropped the tumbler on to the floor and, picking it up again, said, 'Behold, not broken. Not even a crack. Even on an uncarpeted floor and certainly not on a rich Aubusson carpet, or noise enough to awaken a sleeper in another bedroom.'

He paused, frowning. 'I suspect that the two ladies, overanxious to endorse the evidence of an unknown intruder, indulged in a little embroidery of the true facts. True, the glass on the kitchen door was broken. But by whom?'

Brodie looked puzzled. 'Why, the intruder of course.'

Faro shook his head. 'Think again, Sergeant. You have already described your search that morning, treading very carefully to avoid shattered fragments of broken glass. And we have Duncan's statement about having to clear up all the pieces – off the grass. Very inconvenient, but very convenient for Mr Fanshaw's killer who we can only presume was ignorant of the laws of gravity.'

At Brodie's bewildered expression, Faro continued: 'When a window glass is broken from the outside the fragments will fall into the room, while a glass shattered with a mighty blow from inside, perhaps using a hammer, will fall to the outside. A deduction somehow overlooked in the original evidence.'

Brodie shook his head, murmuring, 'I don't understand . . .'

Faro went on: 'All the evidence points to one thing and one

thing only, Sergeant. And that is that our vanishing vagrant was a convenient invention—'

'Excuse me, sir, I saw him and so did Mrs Dora and Duncan. It's in the statements.'

Faro held up his hand. 'Sergeant, all you saw was someone you were meant to see. Someone dressed to look like a vagrant. Your careful observation about the boots was the first clue.'

Brodie did not look convinced. 'He could have stolen them—'

'One moment, Sergeant. You did not actually see him leap over the back wall, did you now?'

'No, sir, he was too quick for me. As for Duncan—'

Faro interrupted, 'But take a moment and consider if you will, any other means of apparently vanishing into thin air.'

Brodie shook his head again and Faro went on: 'It is quite simple really, Sergeant. While you were struggling to unlatch the gate our vagrant had slammed shut, he dashed into the kitchen, the door having been left open for this purpose . . .' Pausing, he continued grimly, 'The murder of Ronald Fanshaw was no tragic result of a break-in by an unknown intruder, Sergeant. It was a matter of utmost planning and execution. That was why it was essential for you and others to get a glimpse of him – from a safe distance.'

'I still don't understand,' Brodie protested.

'Then let me tell you. Mrs Dora, something of an actress, took on the guise of the vanishing vagrant and either she or Mrs Wade, or both of them, were guilty of Fanshaw's murder.'

At their next meeting, Faro told Winton of his findings; the doctor congratulated him and then solemnly produced his trump card.

'On her death bed, Mrs Wade told me that Dora and her Peter had been in love for years. Peter, the illegitimate son with Ronald squandered the fortune he believed was rightfully his as well as Dora's inheritance. Fanshaw's cruelty was the last straw, so Mrs Wade took matters into her own hands. She insisted that Dora was innocent.

'Doctor-patient confidentiality, Faro, but I wanted to see you solve the mystery yourself. You didn't disappoint me and I believe your version is nearer the truth. Dora's abilities as an actress were essential to the plot. They got away with murder, but no one would ever be able to prove it.'

No one, except Inspector Faro. But it was only for his own and Winton's satisfaction. The main participants were dead and the case of the vanishing vagrant would remain in police files as murder by person or persons unknown.

DECK THE HALLS WITH POISON, IVY

Susan Moody

Susan Moody published her first crime novel in 1984 and later chaired the Crime Writers' Association. She also served as President of the International Association of Crime Writers. In addition to mysteries, she has also published historical fiction.

When her sister picked up the phone, Veronica Lewis said, 'What time will you arrive at Mother's for Christmas?'

'I'm not going to Mother's for Christmas,' Teresa said.

'What?'

'I already told you that,' said Teresa patiently. 'Several times.'

'But why not?' Although Veronica already knew the answer, she couldn't resist the question.

'Because every year,' Teresa said, 'every *single* year, Mother's managed to ruin Christmas for me and my family. Now the worm has turned.'

'Aren't you forgetting that this is the season of goodwill to all men?'

'Mother is not a man. I sometimes wonder if she's even a human being.'

'Well,' Veronica said, 'I'm not going to go without you there.'

'And I'm not going, period.'

Ivy Lewis carried the box of Christmas decorations down from the attic. She loved Christmas. These days, you could buy peaches in January and strawberries in March, but Christmas was different. Christmas decorations only appeared at Christmas time, and for the rest of the year were put away. Which was how it should be.

And the best bit of Christmas was the tree. Mind you, this year, there'd been a bit of trouble. She'd had to take hers back, at considerable expenditure of time and effort, because when she got it home, the top sprig, on which the final, last-minute angel would be placed, had a definite kink in it.

'It's not the only thing round here with a kink in it,' the man at the yard had said, adding that she must have done it herself, cramming it into her car; it had been perfectly straight when it left his yard, and anyway, she was going to put a fairy on top, wasn't she?

When she shuddered delicately at the thought of anything so vulgar as a fairy, and murmured something about angels, he'd said rudely, 'Angels, fairies, same difference, innit? Point is, you're going to stick it up her backside, so nobody's going to see it anyway.'

So *common* . . . She'd tried to insist that he replace the tree, and he'd said he hadn't any trees left at the price she'd bought hers, only the more expensive ones, and when she refused to pay the extra, he'd told her to get lost. So in the end, she'd had to stuff the original tree back in the car and take it home again.

Her ruffled mood was soothed by her work. Even if they begged, it was a job she'd never let the girls help with, in case they broke something. She loved hanging the crystal icicles, the opalescent glitter-dusted globes, the plaited straw ornaments. She loved squinting into the sides of the silver balls at her own distorted image, enjoying the curve which made her look like some evil old goblin rather than the well-preserved, immaculately turned-out woman of sixty-three which, though she said it herself, she was.

How Teresa and Keith could slop about in slacks and a shirt all day, she really couldn't understand. She'd even said as much to her, last Christmas, but it hadn't made any difference. And as for the children, allowed to appear at the dining table in those uncouth trainers and baggy jeans, well; she'd refused to bring in the turkey until they all went and changed. Christmas comes but once a year, she told them, and when it comes, we try to make a ceremony of it, we try to rise to the occasion.

And it wouldn't have hurt Keith to have made an effort by putting on a tie and jacket, either.

And there was Teresa saying, 'Re*lax*, Mother, for God's sake,' in that tight-lipped way, and sighing heavily when she, Ivy, said that while they were in her house they ought to conform to her standards, no matter what kind of lax behavior was permitted in their own home. And Em, her very own sister, acting in her usual mousey way, fluttering about and trying to get everybody to smile until she, Ivy, had quite understandably snapped at her, which of course made Em dissolve into tears. All of which meant that by the time they'd got the turkey carved – Keith, as usual, making a complete disaster of the job and spilling fat (*so* difficult to remove, as she'd pointed out) all over the lace tablecloth – nobody ate a thing. Ivy had served it up again at suppertime: she wasn't going to see good food going to waste, even though Keith refused to come to the table, preferring to drink himself stupid, as per usual, and Teresa kept telling the children not to worry, they'd soon be home again.

Ivy reached forward with another silver ball. When she had been a child, Christmases were mean and awkward, her mother usually sulking, her father shouting. She'd tried to make everything different for her own children, but a more ungrateful, sullen pair of girls it would have been hard to imagine.

'Hi, Terry, it's me again. Look, if you're not going to Mother's, what are you doing instead?'

'Staying at home with my loving family, Veronica. Where you're welcome to join us.'

'I wish I was as brave as you are.'

'Brave doesn't come into it. It's a matter of survival. Last year, Keith said he'd divorce me if I ever made him spend Christmas at Mother's again. And I said I'd divorce him if he allowed me to. So this Christmas, we shall stay home and eat what we like, when we like. Wear what we like. Spend Christmas in the *bath*, if we feel like it, without all the snide comments about the cost of hot water. Make love in the mornings without Mother knocking on the wall.'

'She's only trying to make things nice for us.'

'What a pity she never succeeds.'

'But she'll be expecting me now.'

'Tell her you've won a cruise to the Balearics and you're going with a boyfriend.'

'What boyfriend?' Veronica said, throbbingly. 'I'm entirely on my own.'

'Have you been drinking?'

'Stop!' shrieked her sister. 'You sound just like Mother.'

'That's the worst insult I've ever had,' said Teresa, laughing. 'I am now going to put down the phone, after which I shall never speak to you again as long as I live.'

'Just before you do, tell me how I'm going to get out of going there for Christmas.'

'Why don't you break a leg? Better still, break two.'

'You're not taking this seriously.'

'I promise you I am. What's more, when I've finished this conversation with you, I'm going to ring her once again and repeat that we're not going to come down. "Mother", I shall say, "every Christmas of my life has been made a hell by your nags and sulks and insults and nastiness. But never again. It's a choice between you and my husband – the husband, I may say, that you did your level best to prevent me from marrying – and I'm afraid my husband wins". And if she tries to argue, I shall just put down the phone.'

'Icy, but polite, huh?'

'Icy, certainly. I shan't bother too much about polite.'

Ivy Lewis replaced the receiver and took a few deep breaths to calm herself. Rage surged inside her, making her heart beat double time, sending an ugly flush into her face. She glanced around and caught sight of herself reflected in the hall mirror. Quickly, she straightened her shoulders, lifted her head, pinned a smile on her face. Heavens above, caught like that, unawares, unprepared, she had almost looked . . . well . . . *old*.

It was typical of Teresa, she thought, to play silly games, hoping Ivy would plead with her. Well (Ivy tightened her lips), she was not going to give her the satisfaction. You'd think she'd be grateful, inviting her and that doltish husband and those ill-disciplined children down every year. The amount of hot water they used was ridiculous, and there were other things. Noises from the bedroom and so forth. Quite blatant noises. When she'd mentioned this to Teresa, however, the girl had jumped down her throat.

'Keith works hard and so do I,' she'd said. 'The time we spend together is very precious to us.'

Ivy had said that she thought Keith could at least restrain himself while he was in his mother-in-law's home but Teresa had flown into a rage.

'Restrain himself?' she'd shouted. 'We're married, for heaven's sake. I know you refused to let poor Daddy touch you once Veronica was born, which is why he finally couldn't take it any more and set up house with nice Barbara from the office, but Keith and I aren't like that, all right?'

Ivy had, frankly, been stunned that Teresa could accuse her own mother of not allowing her father his marital rights. She'd never wanted children in the first place, but she'd done her duty, provided him with the family he had asked for. What more did he want?

And then on top of everything else, Teresa had the unmitigated gall to speak of 'nice Barbara'. Talk about disloyal – but what else could you expect from someone so coarse, which she'd certainly not got from Ivy's side of the family.

The following afternoon, she stood in the wide hallway of her house and looked around. Maybe she would buy a second tree this year – it looked so nice, when people came, to have the little white lights winking. Not that many people *did* come. Good thing, too. Even the vicar didn't call any more, after she'd asked him to leave his shoes outside. It had been raining and she didn't want dirt and mud trodden in. The way he'd reacted! It was probably something to do with being gay. And, of course, when she'd mentioned it to the girls, Teresa had rudely demanded to know why a gay person couldn't do the job as well as a pervert like Father Cyril Parker had been. Celibate, she'd snorted, in that ugly way of hers; it didn't stop him from putting his hand up my skirt, that time he called round and you were out, Mother. Such a terrible thing to say! As if a man in a position of moral responsibility would do such a thing.

Ivy tugged the ladder from its place under the stairs. Hanging the gold stars up on the ceiling was one of her favorite bits of Christmas decoration. They were all different shapes and sizes, attached to varying lengths of cotton and held in place by sticky tape. When they were hanging from the ceiling, the effect was magical. What those girls didn't appreciate was the time and trouble she took to make things nice for them at Christmas time.

'Are you coming to us for Christmas or not?' Teresa asked. 'Auntie Em'll be here. And Dad's coming, too. It'll be the first Christmas he'll have been allowed to spend with his grandchildren.'

'Sounds wonderful,' Veronica said wistfully. 'A real family Christmas. But if I tell Mother I'm not coming to her, she'll ring me day and night until I agree to go after all.'

'Then lie,' her sister said. 'Take the phone off the hook. Get an answering machine.'

'It's all right for you,' wailed Veronica. 'You live miles away and you've got a man to defend you. I haven't.'

'You could have had.'

'Except for Mother's attitude.'

'You should have stood up to her. Stephen was exactly right for you.'

'But a bit of a wimp, to be put off by her.'

'Just a pragmatist. He could see the trouble she'd cause if he married you and he very sensibly moved on. If you'd had the courage to tell her to get knotted, you'd be a happily married woman now.'

The gold stars drifted in the air currents caused by the heat from the radiators and caught the light from outside, throwing bright shadows on to the walls of the hall. It looked wonderful, Ivy thought. She picked up a six-pointed star and reached for the last empty space on the ceiling, right in the corner of the hall. Stretched to the limit of her reach, she pressed the cotton thread with its piece of sticky tape against the plaster. Just as she lowered her arms, the star fell away. She lunged after it, caught it and then found herself falling, her leg jamming between the struts of the ladder, the whole thing crashing down on top of her. Her head hit the tiled floor and she blacked out.

When she came to, it was dark outside. From the sitting room she could hear the sound of some quiz show on the new plasma screen TV she'd bought three months ago. There'd been a real fuss when she accused the man who came to install it of stealing her rings, said she'd call the police if the shop didn't do something about it – and after all that, she'd found them on the kitchen window sill, hidden behind the pot of thyme. She hadn't called the shop back to let them know – she'd have looked so foolish.

There were no lights on and the house felt extremely cold. She tried to get up and found that the slightest movement sent intense pain flooding through her body. My hip, she thought. I've broken my hip. One of her legs was bent at an unnatural angle; when she tried feebly to push away the ladder, she couldn't shift it. The worst thing was not the pain but the cold. Her hands felt like blocks of ice; her feet were numb.

Surely she had not been unconscious for so long that the central heating timer had switched itself off for the night. If she didn't get warmed up soon, and have the doctor look at her, she might . . . she might even *die*.

The possibility hovered over her in the dark hallway like a giant bird of prey.

But someone would be bound to come. The mailman, for instance. She could shout, when he pushed open the letter box to put the letters through. An appalling thought struck her. That would mean lying like this, in the cold and the dark and pain, until somewhere around eight thirty or nine o'clock in the morning. Even later: this close to Christmas, the postal deliveries were always delayed; she'd had words about it only the other day, called up the local supervisor and complained, said she didn't pay her rates in order not to receive her mail until eleven o'clock in the morning. As it turned out, there had been no mail for her that day, but it didn't alter the fact that it was a downright disgrace.

Suppose the mailman didn't come? She looked over at the telephone. She tried to pull herself forward on her elbows but the pain from her hip was so excruciating that she fell back, her mouth filling with saliva, nausea clogging her throat. The sharp edge of the ladder cut into her neck; she tried to push it away but the effort rammed it against her leg and she screamed aloud. The sound jolted her into more awareness. If she screamed, no one would hear; this was an exclusive residential area and each house was set well apart from its neighbors. If she had moved to a smaller house, as Tom wanted her to when the girls left home, she might have stood more chance of catching someone's attention. That was when he'd asked her to agree to a reduction in alimony payments, but she'd refused. She didn't see why she should subsidize him and Barbara. Not that she was worried about money, because there'd been a very nice sum when her father died and a great deal more when her mother went. It was just the principle of the thing.

Surely, she thought, as the hours went by, Teresa would telephone to say she hadn't meant it, of course she and the children wanted to come for Christmas. Or Veronica. They'd been speaking of it just a couple of days earlier, though Veronica had sounded so reluctant that Ivy had said tartly if Veronica had something better to do, then of course she mustn't feel obliged to spend Christmas Day with her mother, after all, it was expensive getting in supplies for everyone, and if they were all going to behave like spoiled children, it wasn't worth the trouble.

As dawn began eventually to break, her stomach growled, reminding her that she hadn't eaten for some time. And her throat was as dry as a desert. Merely thinking about it made it even dryer so that she began coughing, and then choking. At the back of her throat was an iodine taste she recognized as blood.

She must have lapsed into unconsciousness again. The telephone woke her from some deep state of non-being. She guessed that it was now the afternoon. Above her head the gold-paper stars drifted gently. At least the heat had come on again, though the hall tiles were still freezing cold. She screamed, startled at the weakness of her own voice, as though hoping that whoever was at the other end would hear her.

After a while, the answering machine kicked in and she heard her sister Em's voice, hesitantly explaining that she wouldn't be able to come down for Christmas this year, she had to . . . erm . . . spend the . . . erm . . . holiday with an old friend who was . . . erm . . . very ill.

Em had never been any good at lying and Ivy knew she was lying now. What old friend? Ivy wanted to shout. You haven't *got* any friends. But Em had put down her phone.

There were no letters lying on the doormat. So even if the postman had come, she would have missed him. There was no milkman either, to leave his pint outside and so perhaps alert the neighbors to the fact that it had not been taken in. She'd rung the dairy so many times to complain that the milkman was cheating her by adding several pints on to each month's total that the dairy had refused to go on supplying her.

Slowly the hall darkened again, as she fell in and out of consciousness.

She woke to hear the back door handle being rattled, then the door being forced open. Two dark shadows tiptoed into the hall. 'Looks like the old bat's gone out,' someone whispered.

'Sitting room's over there,' said the other. 'You get the TV, the video, the silver on the sideboard; we'll take the microwave when we leave. You start loading up the van while I nip upstairs and see if there's any jewellery worth taking.'

Ivy watched him from the corner of the hall. In the dark, he didn't notice her. She wanted to call out for help, but between her fear and her thirst and the dryness of her throat, she couldn't get the words out. Couldn't even manage so much as a whimper. When he came downstairs again, he was carrying the small three-drawer jewelry chest which held her good things, and as he came quietly across the tiles, she recognized him immediately: it was the man from the shop where she'd bought the new TV.

'Serve her right, the vindictive old bat,' he said, nodding at his mate, who was carrying the big plasma screen TV. 'Pure poison, she is, never has a good word for anybody, and talk about mean . . . Lost me my job, she did.'

'Been out of work since then, haven't you?'

'That's right. The kids aren't going to have much of a Christmas this year, I can tell you.'

'Maybe we'll get a good price for this little lot.'

'Hope so. Vicious old bat.' As he went past the ladder, he kicked it hard; Ivy fainted again from the pain. She heard the men go out through the back door and the sound of a van starting up.

The phone woke her again. After eight rings, the answering machine kicked in. 'Mother? It's Veronica. I'm terribly sorry, but I'm not going to be able to come for Christmas after all. I have to go away for the . . . the whole week. I'd thought I'd better let you know now, before you go out and buy the turkey.'

'Help!' Ivy croaked.

'I'm really sorry, Mother. But I'll definitely get over to see you before the New Year, all right?'

'Help me!'

But Veronica didn't choose to answer. She'd always been like that, totally selfish and self-obsessed. Even semi-conscious, Ivy could tell that like Em, she was lying, just like that business with Father Parker – or was that Teresa? It didn't matter.

Ivy tried to lick her dry lips but her tongue was equally dry. Her throat was swollen. She was having difficulty focusing her mind, but she thought she must have been lying on the floor for several days now, unable to move. *And* she'd soiled herself.

'Well, I did it! Rang Mother and told her I couldn't make it for Christmas. And so far, she hasn't rung me back to start arguing.'

'So we'll expect you for lunch, shall we?'

'With bells on. I can't wait. I'll go down and see her afterwards.'

At midday on December 27, Veronica Lewis rang the doorbell of her mother's house. After a while, she rang again. She knocked as well. Then she stepped back and looked up at the bedroom windows. No drawn curtains, no lights left on. She tried to peer through the letter box but Ivy had covered it with a piece of felt, in case the local hooligans tried to push dog excrement through.

When Veronica said that was highly unlikely, Ivy had pursed her lips. 'Young people today – they've got no respect for others.'

After a while, Veronica pulled out her cell phone and dialed her mother's number. She could hear the phone ringing inside the house and then the answering machine kicking in. Was Mother out shopping? Veronica had left a message earlier to say she would be coming down.

Perhaps Ivy had gone out, just to punish her, to make her feel even more guilty than she already did, though she'd phoned every day, hoping to wish Mother a happy Christmas.

But really it had been such fun this year, the kids happy for once, and Keith singing a funny song and all of them creased with laughter at Dad's jokes, and Barbara gathering the children round her and reciting 'Twas the Night Before Christmas' from memory, like a real grandmother, instead of getting at them all the time.

Veronica dialed once more. There was still no response, and when she peered through the leaded-glass insert in the front door, all she could make out was the stars which hung from the ceiling, twinkling and shining, and Ivy's coat, or a garbage bag or something, lying on the hall tiles.

Relieved, she went back to her car and drove away. She'd drop by again later.

FROM MINOR TO MAJOR

A Case for Jack Colby

Amy Myers

Amy Myers has written many crime and historical novels, and is currently at work on a new series featuring Jack Colby, in collaboration with her husband Jim. Jack is a car detective, working with a specialist Kent police crime unit when he is not at Frogs Hill Classic Car Restorations.

'It's me, Jack. I'm back in town.'

That was the first phone call I had had from Matt Redwell in well over thirty years. We'd been childhood chums of a sort – the sort you're sneakily glad to be rid of, which had been especially so in Matt's case.

'Heard you run some sort of repair shop, Jack. Might bring my Morris Minor in for you to give it a going over.'

To hear Jack Colby's Frogs Hill Classic Car Restorations so described set my gears grinding. We do not give cars a 'going over'. We patiently and lovingly restore them to their former glory. But I couldn't say no to Matt Redwell, and mustered what cordiality I could.

'Bring it in, Matt.'

He brought the Minor in, and a sorry sight it was – rust, faded paint, you name it. I set my trusty team of two to work, and after they had crawled over it, fixing everything from sloppy gearbox to perished wheel bearings, he came to Frogs Hill to collect it.

'Good job,' he said, casting a casual eye over its now immaculate appearance. 'How much do I owe you, Jack?'

I nerved myself up for my grand confession. 'Nothing. I owed *you*.'

He blinked a bit but didn't comment, so I explained.

'Remember when you lost your Dinky post office van? Well, it was me who nicked it, and I still feel bad about it.' An understatement. It had nagged uneasily at the back of my mind ever since.

Matt gave me what one might call a sideways glance, nodded his thanks, and drove off, together with the albatross of guilt that had been hanging round my neck. I'd lost sight of that Dinky van over the years along with several others in my childhood collection, including a treasured Dinky Ford GT40. But that's life, and now I was free of Matt for good. Or so I had thought.

The second phone call was rather different.

'Jack? It's me, Matt.'

'What's up?' I asked cautiously.

'I am. For murder.'

No joke. A white-faced Matt came hurtling along to Frogs Hill in the Minor to tell me he was out on police bail for murdering his wife and I was his first port of call for help in proving his innocence.

'Why me?' I asked. I didn't like the sound of this.

'Heard you're a car detective.'

'Right. But I hunt down stolen cars, not murderers.'

He sounded hurt. 'But you owe me, Jack . . .'

I looked at him, I looked at the Morris Minor, remembered all our careful work on it, sighed and surrendered. With the Matt Redwells of this world logic doesn't work.

I'd read about the case – who hadn't? A row had broken out at a Greek taverna by the River Medway. An initially unnamed woman had been stabbed, her husband arrested for murder. There had been heavy press hints that there was more to it than that.

'I'll have a nose around,' I told him reluctantly.

'That's good, because I've already fixed it with Dimitri. The taverna's closed on Tuesdays so he'll see you then. The other four are coming too. I told them it's a sort of reconstruction, but I know it was one of them who killed my Shelley. Should be simple enough to work out which.' He gazed at me hopefully.

I must have missed something. 'What four? And why aren't you coming?'

Matt looked as near embarrassed as his jaunty cocky self would permit. 'There were six of us there that night and I'm not coming because they said there was no way they'd talk to a murderer, meaning me. I know what they're up to. They'll convince you I did it. I know that lot.'

'You'd better tell me what the police have on you.'

He shuffled a bit. 'It's not good,' he admitted. 'I found Shelley's body, but did a damn fool thing. Shock, I suppose. Pulled the skewer out of her and got blood on me.'

My stomach suggested I wasn't going to like this story. 'Skewer?' I asked weakly.

'One of those metal things – we'd all ordered kebabs that night.' Matt sounded as matter-of-fact as though death by such means was a natural consequence. 'About a foot long. They had biggish heat-resistant tops to them and they found my fingerprints all over them. Only *my* fingerprints, so they'll find only my DNA too, most like. Trouble is,' he added, 'Shelley and I had had a flaming row, which doesn't help.'

How could I put this? 'Otherwise your relationship with Shelley was good?'

He considered this. 'No, can't say it was. How would you like to be married to a rampant nympho? Sex among a few friends is one thing, throwing it around is a different ball game.'

I'd been right. I didn't like this story. 'Take it from the beginning, Matt.'

'Right. OK. The six of us – we call ourselves the Sextet – have been going to Dimitri's Taverna for yonks. It's our regular.'

'For what?'

'Give me a break, Jack. For sex, of course. *Sex*tet. Short for Sex-Tête-à-Tête only it weren't our heads knocking together. See?'

I did. And I liked the story even less. It was going to be one heck of a repayment for nicking one Dinky toy when I was nine years old.

'I'll tell you like it was,' Matt offered. 'Shelley and me

went in the Morris Minor, Tony and Rose in their Morris
Major, Sue and Rob in their thirties' Bentley. We did the
regular draw during the meal; the three women each picked
a car out of the hat, then the three men did.'

'And guess what,' I finished for him. 'You would all drive
back with the allotted drivers and passengers for each car and
take a nightcap at an agreed home.'

'Yeah. Only this night we didn't get that far, because it all
went wrong. We did the draw after the *mezze* but Shelley and
me both picked the Minor and she started shouting the odds
at being stuck with me. Sue was upset at being paired off with
Rose's hubby Tony and not me, Rob kicked up a fuss because
Tony's a rotten driver and he was worried about his Bentley,
and Rob and Rose were in the Major, which set me off, because
I fancied Rose and I was stuck with Shelley.'

I gulped, marvelling at the way some people take their
pleasures. 'That kind of situation must have cropped up before,
though.'

'True enough, Jack, but that evening Shelley and me were
seriously on the outs. We'd had this row the way over because
she was spreading her wings far and wide, if you know what
I mean.'

Again, I did. It wasn't difficult.

'We were at a table in the garden, and during the kebabs
the next row broke out. Shelley preferred the Bentley with
Rob driving it, and she made her feelings loud and clear that
she wasn't going to put up with third best man, her loving
husband, and that the vote had been rigged. Shelley was right
actually. *I had* rigged it, but I must have mucked it up, and it
looked bad for me when the police heard that. None of us was
happy and while we polished off the kebabs the row got worse
and the noise level shot up.

That brought Dimitri over to the table. He couldn't get a
word in edgeways for a while and stood there fuming over
what to do about it. He told Stavros – he's the waiter – to
clear our plates away and then kick off the Greek dancing on
the terrace earlier than usual so that we could do our shouting
and yelling up there. Stavros always starts it off, because he
does the best jumping around. He's a good-looking lad and

flaunts what he's got, so it gets the ladies going. Shelley said it couldn't start soon enough for her because what she wanted was a real man, not one out of a hat, and off she marched to the terrace, did a twirl or two with Stavros and the other customers began to gather, along with us.'

'Fascinating,' I murmured. It sounded a nightmare. 'What happened next?'

'Dimitri's plan was a good one and I thought we'd all cool off. The non-drivers amongst us were all tanked up on Dimitri's Greek plonk, and the Greek zither and lyra music was blaring over the sound system, and there was Stavros doing his Zorba act while we all circled around him. Once we got going, everyone started having a good time again. When Dimitri called time at eleven o'clock, we all paid our bills and came back for the final dance with Stavros doing his stuff. I'd swear Shelley was there then, but when it ended I couldn't see her. I assumed she was in the toilets and hung around; the others wanted to get away and Sue said Shelley hadn't been in the loo so I went to join the others in the car park thinking she might have shot off in the Minor in a huff to leave me stranded. But the Minor was still there. So back I went.

'I did find her this time, and it wasn't pleasant, I can tell you.' He gulped. 'I panicked. I could see she was dead and I . . . well, I remembered the good times we'd had and all that. Dammit, Jack, I loved her even though I wanted to kick her to kingdom come and back –' he caught sight of my expression – 'not literally,' he added hastily. 'It was seeing her like that, Jack, that's what made me act so stupid. There wasn't much blood on her when I first saw her because the skewer was still in but she can't have been dead for long because when I pulled it out, I got some on me. I must have yelled a bit, because Dimitri turned up and called the police.'

It didn't look good for Matt – and that meant it didn't look good for me. I could feel that albatross round my neck again.

Dimitri's Taverna was tucked away at the end of a lane leading down to the river, and had of course been thoroughly checked out by the police. By Tuesday I heard nothing through my police contacts that suggested their searches had yielded any other thesis than that Matt Redwell was guilty of Shelley's murder. He'd killed her on the spur of the moment and shock made him stay put and then pull the weapon out.

I arrived on the early side in the hope of having a scout round and chat with Dimitri before the other four arrived. It didn't look a large establishment but the prices on the menu seemed to compensate for that. Certainly it was a pretty spot. The front of the taverna had a view over the river, but the gardens where the Sextet had been sitting last week were behind the building, as was the terrace. The car park was on the far side of the lane opposite the garden and I was able to walk straight through the gate and have a quick look around. The toilets were to my left, a modern extension to the restaurant, which looked as if it had been converted from two or maybe three cottages.

The garden looked delightful, with a central path and tables on either side; each one was screened by tall bushes for privacy. I had gathered from Matt that Dimitri was not only Mine Host but also the chef with Stavros as live-in waiter, and someone who could only be Dimitri himself came striding towards me – dark-haired, moustache, and a brash confidence that the Greeks put over so convincingly. I almost expected him to strike a pose and start dancing, but he didn't. He must be in his forties and probably left all flaunting to Stavros.

Dimitri regarded me with deep suspicion. 'So,' he said, 'you think we kill our customers here, eh, Mr Colby?'

'I hope not,' I replied amicably. 'I'm just here to find out what happened and need your help.'

He glared at me. 'I help you see it was Mr Redwell who killed that lovely lady. I will show you where she lay dead.'

He led me towards the gate, but turned before we reached it into another bush-secluded area. This one did not have a table in it, but several benches around the sides, each with a low coffee table before it. In the grassy centre I could see the remains of police chalk marks which brought the reality of murder very near.

'Here we serve drinks to customers who wait for tables to be cleared,' Dimitri told me.

'So what was Shelley Redwell doing here so late in the evening?'

'She liked gentlemen, Mr Colby. Any gentleman.'

'But why linger in here? She was in a party with three of them.'

'I do not know.'

Fair enough. 'She can't have been dead for very long before you found Mr Redwell with her body.'

'No,' he said simply. 'He only just killed her, that's why. Passion, Mr Colby. Drinks, drugs, knives; this is a bad world.'

Noises from the car park suggested the remaining Sextets had arrived, less Matt of course. I don't know quite what I expected. They certainly weren't wearing labels reading Sex Maniac; they looked like four adults tired after a day's work. It was easy to pick out who was who from the descriptions Matt had given me. Rob was tall, rather serious-looking, his wife Sue a long-haired blonde with a supercilious air; Tony was shorter and pugnacious; and the demure dark-haired witch at his side was Rose whose dancing brown eyes made me see why Matt fancied her.

'You know what Matt's up to in sending us along to meet you,' Tony began belligerently. 'You're in with the Old Bill, aren't you, so he's hoping you'll accuse one of us of having killed Shelley.'

'Only if it's the truth,' I said mildly.

'And who decides that?' Sue asked imperiously.

'The police. Look,' I said, 'I owe Matt a favour which is why I'm here. I just want you to tell me what happened and where. It could have been more or less anyone on the terrace at the end of the evening, as far as I can see. There were other customers as well as you six.'

A look flashed amongst them, and they all quickly agreed with this diagnosis. Dimitri noticed it too. 'I call Stavros,' he said firmly. 'He there, he help.'

'Good idea,' Sue said, rather too quickly. Perhaps Matt was wrong about his being her preferred date.

Summoned by Dimitri's walkie-talkie, Stavros rapidly appeared. Good-looking he certainly was, but the sullen expression and the impatient flicks of his elegant hips indicated that he was not happy about being here, even when Sue edged nearer to him. And then I began the reconstruction, feeling somewhat out of my depth. I reconstruct cars not murders, but I supposed that the principle was the same: study the whole, pick out the flaws, apply logic.

Rob led the way over to the table where the party had sat that night. It had a sad look because the crime scene had only just been lifted and the chairs looked as though they remained just as they had been left when the Sextet sprang up to rush to the terrace.

'This is all rubbish,' Rob said impatiently. 'Shelley wasn't murdered until well after eleven o'clock. What's the point of going through this rigmarole of what happened earlier?'

'Every point,' Tony retorted. 'This is where Matt got riled up enough to kill her. The draw went wrong. Shelley didn't want Matt, and that started it all off.'

This emphasis on Matt seemed to give the others confidence and they grew more cooperative. An imaginary draw took place, imaginary dishes were delivered, Dimitri arrived, and then a sulky Stavros removed the imaginary empty plates. It didn't tell me a lot, but I pretended it did by nodding sagely.

'I'm told Shelley really wanted you, Rob,' I said. 'Was that OK by you?'

'No way,' he said hastily as Sue looked at him suspiciously.

'Rob hated the idea, didn't you, darling?' she cooed.

'Shelley wanted the Bentley,' Tony growled. 'Not Rob.'

'Thanks, Tony,' Rob snapped. 'Anyway, Matt took the hump and began yelling at her.'

'Was there any suggestion that the draw result should be changed?'

The four seemed uncertain about this, so Dimitri decided to join in. 'Mrs Redwell say she not happy. She not want man drawn out of hat.'

That was true, the four speedily agreed, led by Rob, I noticed. Nevertheless, so far it was a fairly united front, and I needed to break it if I was going to save Matt – if of course he was innocent. I plunged into battle again.

'So you sent Stavros back to the kitchen with the plates, Dimitri. Were the skewers on them?'

'I do not remember that,' Stavros answered.

'Does anyone?' I asked.

Apparently not. I was stuck in the slow lane and I needed to pull out and get moving if I was to overtake the opposition.

'Then I begin dancing.' Stavros illustrated the point for us with a sophisticated twirl. 'Mrs Redwell comes up to join me and the others followed.'

'Very keen on Greek dancing was Shelley,' Tony said meaningfully, with a slight pause before the word 'dancing'.

Dimitri got the message. 'You thinking Stavros killed the lady? Not possible. I call for the finish at eleven o'clock; I get them to pay bills, and then they go out to have a final dance. Stavros there all the time.'

'What then?' I asked.

'I go to kitchen to do washing up like Dimitri tell me,' Stavros chimed in crossly, clearly seeing this as an unmanly role. 'He see me there,' he added, and Dimitri nodded.

'Were you all present during the final dance?'

'Yes,' Sue said firmly.

'Except for Shelley,' Tony said. 'I told the police that. She was there during part of it, but not right at the end. She could only have been gone for a minute or two. I thought she had gone to the loo.'

'All of you see Matt at the end?' I asked.

Silence. 'I did,' Rose said firmly, and the others reluctantly agreed.

'But while Matt was barging around looking for her I reckon he saw poor Shelley in that hidey-hole waiting for someone, and lost his cool,' Rob said.

'But which one of you would she have been waiting for? According to the draw, it was Matt, but she wouldn't be having a rendezvous with him,' I pointed out.

'Not me,' Tony said. 'Anyway, the draw was more or less off because of all the rows. Rose was with me all the time back at the car park, weren't you, love?' She nodded.

'Nor me,' Rob put in hastily. 'Sue and I were in the car park too.'

Tony looked puzzled. 'No, as we left, I saw Sue follow Stavros back into the taverna.'

Sue flushed. 'I had a quick word with him about dancing lessons.'

'Of course,' Rose said sweetly, 'you do love Greek dancing, don't you?' What Sue really liked was quite clear.

'Matt said you checked the toilets, Sue, to see if Shelley was there,' I said.

Sue grew even redder. 'Well, she wasn't, was she? What does it matter where I was? I wasn't killing Shelley.'

But Rob might have been, I thought – until he dashed my hopes. 'And before you jump to any conclusions, Mr Colby,' he said, 'I should explain that as Tony and Rose will confirm I walked back with them to the car park, and Sue joined shortly afterwards.'

The front was still united.

When I have a duff car engine before me, I can pick out which bit is at fault. Nine times out of ten, it's in the ignition system. I get drawn to it by a kind of instinct, which I can then back up with fact. Faced with the Sextet, however, I didn't seem to be igniting. The only one of the four who could theoretically have killed Shelley was Sue, but I wasn't happy with this deduction. I had no doubt that there were a lot of hidden emotions in this group that I wasn't going to get to hear about, but had they led to murder? A crime of passion, Dimitri had called it, but that didn't tell me whose passion it was.

My engine seemed to be misfiring in a big way.

That night I dreamed not of hidden passions but of kebabs racing around in a Dinky post office van. Luckily when I awoke my inner engine began to rev up again and I realized I hadn't focused sufficiently on whom Shelley was waiting for. She was hiding from Matt, that was for sure, but that meant she must have plans for later, which did not include him. So that led me – where?

I went on pondering the problem while out on police work over a vanished Triumph Stag, and I took the opportunity to make a few enquiries at police HQ. The DI on Matt's case was surprisingly cooperative – in his own way.

'It was Matt Redwell, you can bank on it. His DNA and prints were on that kebab stick and no one else's. It's a wrap.'

It sounded bad, but then so can a rough idle in a high

performance engine. For me the kebab stick proved the push start I needed.

'Where did he get it from?' I asked.

'Eh?' The DI looked at me as though the car crime unit was wasting taxpayers' money in employing me. 'They all had kebabs for dinner. He kept his back.'

Ignoring the fact that a twelve-inch kebab stick would be an uncomfortable accessory tucked into one's socks while Greek dancing, I pointed out, 'Stavros's prints would be on them too, or the chef's when he transferred them from grill to plate.'

He looked thrown. 'So Redwell picked up a clean skewer from the kitchen. Easy enough, probably.'

'When?'

'After the dancing ended.'

'Unnoticed by Dimitri, Stavros and the lady who was intent on a quick snog with him?'

The DI said he'd think about it, and I went on thinking myself. A crime of passion – and yet there hadn't been much obvious passion in the Sextet's game. Shelley was a lady who spread her favours far and wide and who had declared she wanted a real man not one drawn out of a hat. Not Matt, not Rob, not Tony.

Matt rang at eight thirty the next morning. He'd left four messages on my answering service for me to ring him, but I'd ignored them all yesterday evening. 'How's it going?' he asked eagerly.

'Not bad,' I said. 'I think I've got it.'

It was another couple of weeks before, having passed on my pearls of wisdom to the DI, I got the tip that I was right, and it looked as if charges could be dropped against Matt Redwell. Out of curiosity I treated myself to a trip to the taverna. It wasn't a Tuesday, but there was a notice on the taverna door announcing that it was closed due to illness. The kind of illness that would keep Dimitri safely behind bars for some consider-able time.

It turned out that he and Shelley had been an item for some

while, but she had just called the whole thing off. That night she made it all too clear she favoured young Stavros and had dashed after him to suggest a rendezvous later. She would hide from Matt in the arbour, and wait for Stavros. But Dimitri's hopes had risen when he heard her make it clear that she was after better game than Matt, but then his pride took a hammering when he heard the assignation being planned with Stavros. So after the final dance he packed Stavros off to the kitchens and went to the arbour himself having earlier provided himself with a kebab skewer and an oven glove to handle it with. The only person who had time and opportunity to do so. Thus equipped, Dimitri had avenged the blow to his manly pride.

To give Matt his due, he came round to thank me before leaving town.

'Knew I could count on you, Jack. Thanks, I owe you.'

'Let's call it quits for the Dinky post office van,' I said with relief, as the last vestiges of guilt rolled off my shoulders.

'Rightio.' He slid into his newly restored Morris Minor, wound down the window and grinned. 'By the way, Jack, did I ever tell you I pinched your Dinky Ford GT40?'

THE UNKNOWN CRIME
Sarah Rayne

Sarah Rayne was educated in Staffordshire, where she still lives, and worked in the property business before establishing herself as a leading writer of psychological thrillers including *House of the Lost*.

I've never been a high-profile thief. I'd better make that clear at the start. But I'm moderately prosperous and over the years I've developed my own line in small, rare antiques. An elegant chased silver chalice from some obscure museum, perhaps, or a Georgian sugar sifter.

But I've always had a yen to commit a crime that would create international headlines. The removal of the Koh-i-noor or St Edward's Crown or a Chaucer first folio. You're probably smiling smugly, but there are people who will pay huge sums of money for such objects. (I'd be lying if I said the money didn't interest me.)

And then my grandfather died, leaving me all his belongings and the dream of a theft that would echo round the world and down the years suddenly came within my grasp.

He lived in Hampstead, my grandfather, and the solicitors sent me the keys to the house. I didn't go out there immediately; I was absorbed in a delicate operation involving the removal of a Venetian glass tazza from a private collection – very nice, too. A saucer-shaped dish on a stem, beautifully engraved. So between tazzas and fences (yes, they *do* still exist as a breed and I have several charming friends among the fraternity), it was a good ten days before I went out to Hampstead. And the minute I stepped through the door I had the feeling of something waiting for me. Something that could give me that elusive, longed-for crime.

I was right. I found it – at least the start of it – in a box of old letters and cards in the attic. I know that sounds hackneyed, but attics really are places where secrets are stored and Rembrandts found. And, as my grandfather used to say, if you can't find a Rembrandt to flog, paint one yourself. My father specialized in stealing jewellery, but my grandfather was a very good forger. He was just as good at replacing the real thing with his fakes. If you've ever been in the National Gallery and stood in front of a certain portrait . . . Let's just say he fooled a great many people.

At first look the attic wasn't very promising. But there was a box of papers which appeared to have been my great-grandfather's. He was a bit of a mystery, my great-grandfather, but there's a family legend that he was involved in the theft of the Irish Crown Jewels in 1907. My father used to say he had never been nearer the Irish Crown Jewels than the pub down the road, but I always hoped the legend was true. And it has to be said the Irish Crown Jewels never were recovered.

It wasn't the Irish Crown Jewels I found in that house, though. It was something far more intriguing.

Most of the box's contents were of no interest. Accounts for tailoring (the old boy sounded as if he had been quite a natty dresser), and faded postcards and receipts. But at the very bottom of the box was a sheaf of yellowing notes in writing so faded it was nearly indecipherable.

How my grandfather missed those papers I can't imagine. Perhaps he never went up to the attics, or perhaps he couldn't be bothered to decipher the writing. If your work is forging fine art and Elizabethan manuscripts, it'd be a bit of a busman's holiday to pore over faded spider-scrawls that will most likely turn out to be somebody's mislaid laundry list or a recipe for Scotch broth.

But the papers were neither of those things.

They were an account of great-grandfather's extraordinary activities during the autumn of 1918.

October, 1918

I've been living in an underground shelter with German shells raining down at regular intervals for what feels like years, although I believe it's actually only three weeks. But whether it's three weeks or three days, it's absolute hell and I'd trade my virtue (ha!) to be back in England.

You'd expect a battlefield to be cut off from the rest of the world, but we get some news here: how the Germans have withdrawn on the Western Front, how the Kaiser's going to abdicate, even how a peace treaty is being hammered out. It's difficult to know what's true and what's propaganda, though. And then last night I was detailed to deliver a message a couple of miles along the line.

I'm not a coward, but I'm not a hero either and it doesn't take a genius to know that a lone soldier, scurrying along in the dark, is a lot more vulnerable than if he's in a properly-dug trench, near a gun-post. But orders are orders and I delivered the message, then returned by a different route. That's supposed to fool the enemy, although I should think the enemy's up to most of the tricks we play, just as we're up to most of theirs.

I was halfway back when I saw the chateau. The chimes of midnight were striking in the south and there was the occasional burst of gunfire somewhere to the north. It was bitterly cold and I dare say I was temporarily mad or even suffering from what's called shell shock. But I stood there for almost an hour, staring at that chateau. It called out to me – it beckoned like Avalon or Valhalla or the Elysian Fields.

I was no longer conscious of the stench of death and cordite and the chloride of lime that's used to sluice out the trenches. I could smell wealth: paintings, silver, tapestries . . .

But I can't drag a Bayeux tapestry or a brace of French Impressionists across acres of freezing mud. Whatever I take will have to be small. And sellable. There's no point in taking stuff that hasn't got a market. I remember the disastrous affair of the Irish Crown Jewels . . .

That's as far as I read that first day. The light was going and the electricity was off, and it's not easy to decipher a hundred-year-old scrawl in an attic in semi-darkness. Also, I had to complete the sale of the tazza. That went smoothly, of course. I never visualized otherwise. I'm very good at what I do. That night I celebrated with a couple of friends. I have no intention of including in these pages what somebody once called the interesting revelations of the bedchamber; I'll just say when I woke up I was in a strange bed and I wasn't alone. And since one can't just get up and go home after breakfast in that situation, (*very* ungentlemanly), it was a couple of days before I returned to great-grandfather's papers.

November, 1918

For two weeks I thought I wouldn't be able to return to the chateau. You can't just climb out of the trenches and stroll across the landscape at will.

Then last night I was chosen to act as driver for several of the high-ranking officers travelling to Compiègne, and I thought – that's it! For once the British army, God bless it, has played right into my hands. I'll deposit my officers in Compiègne, then I'll sneak a couple of hours on my own.

We set off early this morning – it's 10 November, if anyone reading this likes details.

Later

I have no idea where we are, except that it's in Picardie. I've been driving for almost an hour and it's slow progress. We've stopped at an inn for a meal; the officers are muttering to one another and glancing round as if to make sure no one's listening.

I'm in the garden, supposedly taking a breath of air, but actually I'm staring across at the chateau and writing this. I can see the place clearly, and it's a beautiful sight.

I was interrupted by the phone ringing. A furtive voice asked if it had the right number and, on being assured it had, enquired if I would be interested in discussing a jewelled egg recently brought out of Russia. Yes, it was believed to be Fabergé. No, it was not exactly for sale, simply considered surplus to requirements. A kindness, really, to remove it.

'Considered surplus by whom?'

'A gentleman prepared to pay very handsomely. He could see you in an hour.'

I hesitated. On the one hand I had great-grandfather's exploits. On the other was the lure of a Fabergé egg.

Fabergé won. Thieves have to eat and pay bills like anyone and I had recently bought a very snazzy dockside apartment.

I rather enjoyed that job. There were electronic sensors in the floor, so I used a simple block and tackle arrangement, which I slid along by means of a suspended pulley-wheel. I scooped the egg from its velvet bed, stashed it in the zipped pocket of my anorak, then wound the pulley back and hopped out through the window.

The client was a charming and cultured gentleman of complicated nationality and apparently limitless funds, and we celebrated the transaction liberally with vodka and caviar. After that we discussed Chekhov and explored the causes of the Russian Revolution until he fell off the chair while making a toast to the House of Romanov and had to be taken to the local A&E with a fractured wrist.

A&E were busy and we were there all night. But my client was polite and civilized during the whole time.

10 November, 1918

We're all being very polite and civilized during this journey, whatever its purpose might be. We're even being civilized to the enemy – half an hour ago we were overtaken by a car carrying three Germans of unmistakable high rank. I didn't panic until we came upon them a few hundred yards further along, parked on the roadside.

'They've got a puncture,' said the colonel in the back of my car, and told me to stop in case we could help.

'Are you mad, sir?' said the major next to him. 'It'll be a trick. They'll shoot us like sitting ducks.'

'We're all bound for the same place, you fool. There won't be any shooting.'

I don't pretend to have much mechanical knowledge, but I can change a wheel with the best – although it felt strange to do so alongside a man with whose country we had been at war with for four years. I expected a bullet to slam into my ribs at any minute, and I promise you I kept a heavy wrench near to hand. But we got the job done in half an hour, with our respective officers circling one another like cats squaring up for a fight.

I stowed the punctured wheel in the boot.

'Not too close to that case,' said the German driver, pointing to a small attaché case.

'Why? It hasn't got a bomb in it, has it?'

'Oh no,' he said, earnestly. He had better English than I had German.

'It contains a— I have not the word—' He gestured to his own left hand where he wore a signet ring.

'A ring? Signet ring?'

'Signet ring, ach, that is right.'

'From a lady?'

He glanced over his shoulder, and then, in a very low voice he said, 'From the Kaiser. I am not supposed to know, but I overhear . . . It's for the signing of the peace treaty.'

I didn't believe him. Would you? I didn't believe a peace treaty was about to be signed and, even if it was, I didn't believe Kaiser Bill would send his signet ring to seal the document. Nobody used sealing wax and signet rings any longer.

Or did they? Mightn't an Emperor of the old Prussian Royal House do just that? In the face of defeat and the loss of his imperial crown, mightn't he make that final arrogant gesture?

'So,' said the German driver, 'it is to be well guarded, you see.'

I did see. I still didn't entirely believe him, but I didn't disbelieve him. So, when he got back into his car, I reached into that attaché case. I expected it to be locked and it was. But it was a flimsy lock – not what you'd expect of German efficiency – and it snapped open as easily as any lock I ever forced. No one was looking and I reached inside and took out a small square box, stamped with a coat of arms involving an eagle. I put the case quietly in my pocket, got back into the car, and drove on.

Infuriatingly, the next few pages were badly damaged – by the look of them they had been shredded by industrious mice or even rats to make nests. I didn't care if the Pied Piper himself had capered through that attic, calling up the entire rodent population of Hampstead as he went. I needed to know what came next.

Clearly great-grandfather had driven high-ranking officials to that historic meeting in a railway carriage in Compiègne Forest, at which the Armistice ending the Great War was signed. And on the very threshold of that iconic meeting, he had planned to go yomping off to some nameless chateau to liberate it of easily transportable loot! Carrying with him what might be Wilhelm II's signet ring.

I carried the entire box of papers home, but after several hours poring over the disintegrated sections I gave up, and hoped I could pick up the threads in the pages that were still intact.

11 November, 1918

Well! Talk about Avalon and Gramarye! I got into that chateau at dawn, and it was so easy they might as well have rolled out a welcome mat.

And if ever there was an Aladdin's cave . . .

The family who owned it must have left very hastily indeed, because it didn't look as if they taken much with them. The place was stuffed to the gunnels with silver and gold plate, paintings, furniture . . . But I kept to the rule I had made earlier and only took small objects. Salt cellars, sugar sifters, candle snuffers. Some Chinese jade figurines, and a pair of amber-studded snuff boxes. Beautiful and sellable, all of them. I thought, If I survive this war, I shall live like a lord on the proceeds of this.

And so I would have done if the military police hadn't come chasing across the countryside. You'd have thought that with a peace treaty being signed – probably at that very hour – they'd overlook one soldier taking a few hours extra to return to his unit. But no, they must come bouncing and jolting across the countryside in one of their infernal jeeps.

I had the stolen objects in my haversack, and I ran like a fleeing hare. I had no clear idea where I was going and I didn't much care, but I got as far as a stretch of churned-up landscape, clearly the site of a very recent battle. There were deep craters and a dreadful tumble of bodies lying like fractured dolls half-buried in mud. The MPs had abandoned their jeep, but I could see its lights cutting a swathe through the dying afternoon, like huge frog's eyes searching for prey. Prey. Me.

The haversack was slowing me down, so eventually I dived into the nearest crater and lay as still as I could. It was a fairly safe bet they would find me, and probably I would get a week in the glass-house, but if they found the chateau loot I would get far worse than a week in the glass-house. And find it they would, unless I could hide it . . .

I'm not proud of what I did next. I can only say that war makes people do things they wouldn't dream of in peacetime.

There were four dead men in that crater. I had no means of recognizing any of them, partly because they were so covered with mud and partly – well, explosives don't make for tidy corpses. I chose the one who was least disfigured, and tipped the stash into the pockets of his battledress, buttoning up the flaps. He was a sergeant in a Lincolshire regiment. I memorized his serial number.

One last thing I did in those desperate minutes. I slipped the Kaiser's signet ring out of its velvet box and put it on the man's hand.

Then I stood up and walked towards the MPs, my hands raised in a rueful gesture of surrender.

I didn't get a week in the glass-house. I didn't even get forty-eight hours. Armistice was declared at eleven o'clock that morning, and four hours filched by a soldier who had driven the colonel to the signing of the peace treaty was overlooked.

And after the celebrations had calmed down, those of us who had survived had to bury the dead.

They say every story is allowed one coincidence and here's mine. I was one of the party detailed to bury the bodies from that very battlefield where I had hidden. That Lincolnshire sergeant was where I had left him, lying in the mud, his jacket securely buttoned, the signet ring on the third finger of his right hand. I promise you, if I could have got at any of the stuff I would have done, but there were four of us on the task and I had no chance.

But when they brought the coffins out, I watched carefully and I saw my Lincolnshire sergeant put into one with an unusual mark on the lid – a burr in the oak that was almost the shape of England.

The journal ended there. Can you believe that? I felt as if I had been smacked in the face when I realized it and I sat back, my mind tumbling. What had my great-grandfather done next? Had he tried to get into the coffin later? But he couldn't have done. If the signet ring of the last German Emperor had been up for grabs after the Armistice, I would have known. The whole world would have known.

I went back to Hampstead the next morning. I intended to scour that house from cellar to attics to find out if my great-grandfather had recovered the Kaiser's signet ring from the coffin—

I've just re-read that last sentence, and it's probably the most bizarre thing I've ever written. Hell's teeth, it's probably the most bizarre thing anyone has ever written. I hope I haven't fallen backwards into a surreal movie or a rogue episode of *Dr Who* and not noticed.

But there were no more journal pages. Eventually, I conceded defeat, and returned to my own flat. This time I ransacked the few family papers I possessed. I don't keep anything that could incriminate any of us, of course – there's such a thing as loyalty, even though my family are all dead. But there were birth certificates, carefully-edited savings accounts – burglars have to be cautious about investments. Too much money and the Inland Revenue start to get inconveniently interested. My father used to buy good antique furniture; my grandfather invested in gold and silver. I don't know what my great-grandfather did.

There were letters there, as well, mostly kept by my parents out of sentiment, and it was those letters I wanted. I thought there might be some from my great-grandmother and I was right; there were several. Most were of no use, but one was dated September 1920, and attached to it was a semi-order for great-grandfather to report to the HQ of his old regiment. He had, it seemed, been chosen 'at random' to be one of the soldiers who would assist in exhuming six sets of 'suitable' remains from battlefields in France.

Random, I thought, cynically. I'll bet he contrived it, the sly old fox.

The six coffins, said the letter, would be taken by special escort to Flanders on the night of 7 November. A small, private ceremony would take place in the chapel of St Pol, and great-grandfather would be one of the guard of honour.

By that time a pattern was starting to form in my mind, and I unfolded my great-grandmother's letter with my blood racing. It read, 'My dear love . . . What an honour for you to be chosen for that remarkable ceremony. When you described it in your last letter it was so vivid, I felt I was there with you . . . The small, flickeringly-lit chapel, the six coffins, each draped with the Union Jack . . . The brigadier general led in, blindfolded, then placing his hand on one of the coffins to make the choice . . .'

That was when my mind went into meltdown and it was several minutes before I could even get to the bookshelves. Eventually, though, I riffled through several reference books, and in all of them, the information was the same.

'From the chapel of St Pol in Northern France, the Unknown Soldier began the journey to the famous tomb within Westminster Abbey . . . The man whose identity will never be known, but who was killed on some unnamed battlefield . . . The symbol of all men who died in battle no matter where, and the focus for the grief of hundreds of thousands of bereaved . . .'

Great-grandmother's letter ended with the words, 'How interesting that you recognized the coffin chosen as one you had helped carry from that battlefield shortly before the Armistice. I wonder if, without that curious burr, you would have known it? It's a sobering thought that you are probably the only person in the whole world who knows the identity of the Unknown Warrior.'

All right, what would *you* have done? Gone back to your ordinary life, with the knowledge that the grave of the

Unknown Warrior – that hugely emotive symbol of death in battle – contained probably the biggest piece of loot you would ever encounter? The signet ring of the last Emperor of Germany – the ring intended to seal the peace treaty that ended the Great War. Wilhelm II's ring that never reached its destination because a German car had a puncture.

The provenance of that signet ring was – and is – one hundred per cent genuine. It's documented in great-grandfather's journal and great-grandmother's letter. Collectors would pay millions.

It's calling to me, that iron-bound casket, that unknown soldier's tomb that's the focus for memories and pride and grief every 11 November. It's calling with the insistence of a siren's seductive song . . . Because of course it's still in there, that ring, along with the loot taken from the French chateau. It must be, because in almost a century there's never been the least hint of anyone having tried to break into that tomb.

I'm ending these notes now, because I have an appointment. I'm joining a party of tourists being taken round Westminster Abbey. Quite a detailed tour, actually. After I come home I shall start to draw a very detailed map of the abbey. Then I shall make precise notes of security arrangements and guards, electronic eyes, CCTV cameras . . .

HE DID NOT ALWAYS SEE HER
Claire Seeber

Claire Seeber enjoyed a successful career in documentary television as well as working as a freelance feature writer for a number of national newspapers before turning her hand to psychological thrillers such as *Never Tell*.

J eff helped Olivia choose the February book, steering her heavily towards Mary Shelley's *Frankenstein*. There were a few inward groans when Olivia had mumbled her idea at the last meeting. The group preferred modern books: they often enjoyed the *Daily Mail*'s selection, or the ones that chat show couple chose. But actually, they all agreed at the meeting, Shelley had hit on something with the creation of the monster. It was hard to imagine it being written by a woman. And, of course, they were most happy to be at Olivia's house with Jeff on hand, so charmingly attentive.

When the women left that evening, tapping out into the cold, clear night beneath the few stars visible in Chiswick's busy skies, Olivia loaded the dishwasher, wiped all the work-tops down, and went up to bed. Jacqueline had lingered; was taking a particularly long time to finish the oily Chardonnay Jeff had so thoughtfully provided, still simpering with spectacular adoration at his jokes. Olivia didn't worry that they'd think her rude for slipping off; her husband would be happy to see Jacqueline out.

Upstairs Olivia peeped in at her daughter, cleaned her teeth and then checked her son. Her heart turned over to see he'd slipped his thumb into his mouth, a habit long fought. His hair was slightly damp and his face flushed. Olivia turned the radiator down and gently tried to disengage his thumb, checking quickly over her shoulder. By the time Jeff had managed to steer an equally flushed Jacqueline out towards her enormous car, Olivia was asleep. He didn't want to have to, but Jeff woke her anyway. He was off on business for ten days early the next morning.

If you keep still for long enough, do you cease to exist? Olivia wondered as she stared out of the kitchen window. The late snow was melting slowly on the small green lawn until the patch looked rather like the Pacer mints she used to steal from Woolworths as a child. Absently Olivia rinsed the last plate until it shone, gazing at the pathetic leaning ball of raisin eyes and carrots that had once been a snowman, the radio beside her rattling with a phone-in about women being ignored in the bedroom.

'If he doesn't see me as I want to be seen, do I not exist?' moaned a well-spoken academic-type called Miriam. 'Do I simply not count in his eyes?'

The presenter murmured sympathetically and moved on swiftly.

Olivia felt a sudden urge to scream loudly. Instead she staunched the hot tap, sealing off the heat that aggravated the deep welts on her left hand. She stared down at the marks, labels of her own weakness. Her youngest wandered in, treading neat muddy footprints across the spotless floor.

'Can I have some crisps?' she asked, but she was already rifling through the cupboard where they lived, her auburn ponytail sleek against her back.

'Can you see me?' Olivia asked her daughter curiously.

'Dur!' her daughter replied, rustling plastic. 'I'm not blind, Mum, you know. I don't have a white stick.' She chose a packet of prawn cocktail and wandered off again. They were ridiculously pink, Olivia observed vaguely, wiping down the sink. Prawns weren't naturally that pink, were they?

He came home early, before Olivia had a chance to clean the mud off the back step. 'Hello,' she said nervously. 'Good trip?' He checked the kitchen in silence. She held her breath; she thought she'd got away with it – then he opened the back door to check. He looked at her just once, his hand-some face inscrutable. In silence, he went upstairs; in silence he came down again, out of his shirt and tie now, wearing a blue tracksuit with white stripes down the side that showed off his tall frame nicely but was frankly horrible in Olivia's eyes. He wasn't the young boy she'd fancied from afar in the refectory any more; he'd taken up running recently to fight his paunch. She wondered if he thought the stripes would make him go faster. Not that she would offer such a frivolous opinion these days.

Olivia had cleaned the mud up now but it was too late, she knew. She also knew that if she crouched in the corner she only enflamed his rage, enflamed it 'til it bubbled; he saw her rather like a dog, cowering from its master. Well, she was a dog, to him.

'Bitch,' he would snarl, his face contorted until he was positively ugly. So instead she chose to stay still when she recognized the signs.

Now she lay flat on the gleaming kitchen floor. She lay flat but her head felt fuzzy.

'What the hell are you doing?' he scoffed, opening the fridge and helping himself to a pork pie. It was very sturdy and compact, Olivia noted from her horizontal position. A small, tight structure of pastry, meat and fat.

'I thought I'd save you the bother,' she answered her husband quietly. She could see dirt, some old cat hairs, a bit of fluff stuck in strange yellow muck on the skirting-board. Luckily he never got this low.

Her eldest walked into the room and stopped when he saw her. 'Have you hurt your back again, Mummy?' he asked, but his eyes were anxious. He moved towards her.

'It's a bit sore, sweetie, yes. You go on now,' she forced a smile. 'Get on with your maths. I'll be up in a minute.'

Her husband laughed mirthlessly, throwing his head back, spraying tiny fragments of pork pie across the sparkling worktop.

'Your mother's a daft bint,' he spluttered to his son, eventually recovering himself. When he laughed, his tracksuit top rode up, showing the top of wiry dark red pubic hair. Olivia felt quite nauseous. 'Did you know that, Dan? A daft fucking bint.'

'You shouldn't call her that,' her eldest muttered, his eyes steadfastly on the floor.

Her husband stopped laughing. He stared at his son.

'Well, you shouldn't,' Dan said, a little louder now, his pale face flushing with the effort of challenging his father. 'It's horrible.' He looked up this time, directly at the older man.

'Get out, Dan,' Olivia said quickly, scrambling to her feet. She knew what came next.

As her husband made a lunge for Dan, the remnants of the pork pie smashing on to the shining tiles, Olivia thrust herself in front of her ten-year-old son. 'Go,' she shouted at him. With a stifled sob, he went.

After the beating, a hot-eyed Olivia struggled to hold back the tears – but she wouldn't give him the satisfaction. Long gone where the days when he held her and cried himself, begging for forgiveness. Long long gone.

She had found that if she kept very still he did not always see her. Over time, a long and weary time that eventually amounted to most of her adult life, Olivia realized that this was likely to be her safest option. Not necessarily her salvation, but the best bet laced on a short string of bad ones.

She leant against the worktop trying to quell her shaking; eventually she asked her husband, 'If I leave you, what would you do?'

He regarded her calmly. He picked a bit of pork out of his teeth and spat it on the floor. 'Him, for a start,' he gestured with his head at the door their son had left through. He smirked at her, then trod the pork pie carefully into the small cracks between the terracotta tiles. 'Little shit.'

On his way out of the room he picked up the copy of *Frankenstein* stacked neatly with the cookbooks.

'And this was quite obviously written by her husband,' he snapped, 'stupid bitch'. He chucked the paperback at Olivia's head; she didn't duck quite in time. Then he scooped up the phone to call his great friend Bert. 'Booked the course, you hound?' Jeff barked with laughter at the response, and slammed the door behind him.

Olivia stared down at the squashed pork pie, his words reverberating round her throbbing head. *Him, for a start*. The pork pie reminded her of her wedding breakfast, the time when love and hope meant more than empty promises. He hadn't hit her until a few weeks after the honeymoon. Until they were on the other side of the world; settling in Jakarta for his work. Until she made the wrong rice for his dinner; until she had no one familiar to turn to and no money of her own. Until she could only wander tearfully on the beach, stepping over the coconut leaf offerings outside each Hindu home and wondering what she'd done; already sick and pregnant in the humid nights with her beloved son.

When the book club arrived for their next meeting at Olivia's house, they were surprised that Jeff was out. He was always there, welcoming them, pouring the wine, joshing them gently in the way they loved, flattering them and making them think if only. He took so much more interest than any of their husbands; in fact, sometimes he even suggested the books that Olivia picked to read.

'Lucky Olivia,' they'd sigh. 'Such devotion. Such a family man. And still so handsome too.' Olivia would smile wanly and deep down they'd think stupid cow, she doesn't deserve him, such a cold woman, so difficult to get close to, so thin and brittle. But they put up with her for Jeff. Lovely man.

This cold March night, Olivia had served up a proper treat. Bowls of glistening green olives, sparkling wine, thick pâté and creamy Brie, a plate of crusty home-made-looking pork pies beside dark red tulips as the centrepiece. Olivia seemed different too. She had some colour in her cheeks for once; she didn't look quite so thin and she'd cut her hair to a sleek and shiny bob that hung just above her shoulders. If you looked closely you might have seen the small scar that marked her forehead, the exact shape of a book corner, but her new fringe hid it well.

'I thought Jeff loved your long hair?' Cathy asked quizzically.

'He did.' Olivia took a big sip of her Prosecco. 'But I hated it. So I had it cut right off.'

'And where is he?' Cathy asked girlishly, looking through the open door into the hall as if Jeff might step in at any moment. 'I quite miss him now he's not here.'

'Do you?' Olivia smiled shyly. 'I find it very – quiet now he's away on business.'

'And where's he gone, the naughty man?' asked Jacqueline with a pained fuchsia smile, secretly ruing the two hours she'd spent that afternoon in Hair Flair having her thin hair bouffed.

'Back to Indonesia; they couldn't do without him, they found. He really is a telecommunications expert, it seems.' Olivia drained her wine. 'He might be gone some time.' She picked up the plate of golden pastry with a steady hand, the little handmade leaves on top of each pie curling in the soft electric light, and offered it around. 'Pork pie, anyone?'

Conned

L.C. Tyler

L.C. Tyler was, like Robert Barnard, born in Essex and educated at Oxford University before spending a number of years working abroad. He turned to crime fiction with the critically acclaimed *The Herring Seller's Apprentice* and his latest book is *The Herring on the Nile*.

He'd conned her. Of that much she was certain. The only things she could not work out were how and why.

In the background, the air-conditioning still purred respectfully. Looking out through the plate-glass window, the view was still exactly as it had been the day before: the city she had always lived in, but seen now from twenty-two floors up, its chaotic traffic proceeding slowly and silently along the dusty streets, the palm trees waving gently, the purple and red bougainvillea peeping over the walls. Her wedding dress was still draped carefully over the sofa in the small recess that qualified this as a suite rather than merely a hotel room. All that had changed since yesterday was that she had somehow mislaid her new husband.

She had met him only weeks before. Of course, the first thing that she had done was to run the plan past her friend, Maria. Maria, for all sorts of reasons, understood the ways of men.

'What's he like?' Maria had asked. She raised her eyebrows inquisitively while sucking up the last of the warm froth at the bottom of her Coca Cola bottle.

'Rich,' she had said.

'And young and tall and handsome?'

'Just rich.'

'Shame,' Maria had said.

'Rich is fine. Good looks aren't important. You're so shallow, Maria, do you know that?'

'That's what they tell me,' Maria had replied. She twirled the bottle, as though wondering whether she had enough coins remaining in her purse for another. 'If he's got money, though, you'd have thought he'd be staying at the Hilton or the Marriott.'

'He says he likes the Casa Blanca. It has lots of local colour. He likes being on the waterfront, by the fish market. He says he can stay in a Hilton anywhere. There's nothing like the Casa Blanca where he comes from.'

'He means it's cheap.'

'You couldn't afford to spend a night at the Casa Blanca.'

'I've spent plenty of nights at the Casa Blanca,' Maria had said.

'I mean, you couldn't afford to *pay* to spend a night there.'

'Does he give you money to sleep with him?'

'Of course not!'

'Just thought I'd check,' Maria had said, putting the empty bottle on the table. 'Go for the long-term approach by all means, if that's what you prefer.'

She opened the wardrobe door. His suit still hung there on a hotel hanger – a hanger cunningly designed so that, if stolen, it would be useless in a normal wardrobe. There was such a lack of trust everywhere these days. She fingered the shiny grey material. It crackled with static electricity. He'd bought the suit especially for their wedding the day before.

'No point in getting anything expensive,' he had said. 'Back home I only shop in Savile Row. Heaps of bespoke suits back home. I don't need any more. I'll just get a local tailor to run me up something. Where does your cousin Carlos get his suits?'

She had pulled a face. 'My cousin's suits look really cheap,' she had said.

'Yes, that's what I thought too,' he had replied.

He had proposed to her after a fortnight, thus disproving Maria's theory that he was just a no-good cheapskate who wanted her for one thing only and wasn't prepared to pay even for that.

'So, he'll take you back to the United States?' Maria had asked.

'To England. He comes from England. The place he lives in is called Finsbury Park – it sounds very beautiful. Finsbury Park. I asked if there were many deer in the park. He said I'd be surprised. We'll be married and live in Finsbury Park, and I will get a British passport.'

'You make sure you do, sugar,' Maria had said. 'And once you have the passport and are living in this park, what will you do then?'

'I thought I'd give him the best three months of his life, then I'd divorce him and take half of his money.'

Maria had nodded. 'Two months should be enough. You don't want to get over-sentimental.'

She checked the chest of drawers. His shirts all seemed to be there. Four shirts in various colours. Half a dozen pairs of socks. One spare pair of underpants. He took a pride in travelling light. Surely if he had walked out on her, he'd have taken his clothes?

Then a sudden panic hit her. She riffled through the top draw again. They'd gone! She took each item of clothing out and shook it, then threw it on the floor. He'd taken them! His passport had gone and so had hers. It was true that she needed her old passport only until she got the new British one – but why should he take that? To stop her following him? And he'd got the ring.

'Has he bought the ring yet?' Maria had asked a few days ago.

'He says that in England it is customary for the bride's family to buy rings for the bride and groom.'

'So you have?'

'My father used his savings. It's an investment, if you like. Once I'm in Finsbury Park and I have my own money, I can pay him back. And I'm going to be bought a really expensive diamond ring as soon as we are in England. He says he knows a . . . what did he call him? . . . "geezer" in Hatton Garden who can get him diamonds really cheaply.'

'The geezer sounds a bit like your cousin, Carlos.'

'Carlos only sells cheap cigarettes. And sometimes whisky. And cocaine, of course.'

'Finsbury Park. Hatton Garden,' Maria had said, dreamily. 'London must be really green.'

'That's what he tells me.'

She sank down on to the bed – the super-king-sized bed that was the main selling point of their suite and that occupied slightly over half the floor space. She'd been a fool. While she was planning to divorce him and take half his money – while she'd almost been feeling guilty about it - he'd been planning all along to swindle her father out of most of his lousy savings and run back to London.

How would she even pay for this room they'd spent one night in? She'd insisted she was not spending her first night as a married woman in the Casa Blanca – it was full of lecherous old men and ladies of doubtful morality. Now she saw this as a mistake. If it had been the Casa Blanca, she felt sure she could have come to some arrangement with the manager – he had been known to do such things – but the manager of this more upmarket hotel would probably insist on payment in some internationally recognized currency. She could be arrested and, if so, she was aware that the local police might have already formed an unfortunate opinion of her virtue and integrity. And what would she tell her parents? She did not often weep, but she did so now. In the process she failed to hear the door being opened. When she looked up he was standing in front of her. He was wearing the slightly stained blazer that he had been wearing when they first met and the same grubby tie with the green and red stripes. He had trimmed his moustache, she noticed, but not well – the pencil-thin line on the right was conspicuously higher than the pencil-thin line on the left. The remains of his hair, once blond, were partly combed over his bald patch, partly hanging loose over his right ear. His beatific smile was enhanced and fully justified by the halo of alcohol that hung around him.

'I realized you'd miss me, lambkin,' he said, 'but I've scarcely been gone more than a couple of hours.'

She looked at her watch. 'Three,' she said.

'I had some business in town,' he said. 'Then I ran into your cousin, Carlos. We stopped for a drink or two. Might have been seven. Clever lad, your cousin.'

'I thought you'd . . . gone,' she said.

'And where would I go without you?' he asked. 'You were asleep. I slipped out without disturbing your slumbers.'

She rubbed the last of her tears away with the back of her hand. She had misjudged him. There would be no unpaid hotel bill, no painful explanations to her parents, no I-told-you-so looks from Maria. Still, it would be as well to proceed with Plan A without further delay. A small quota of guilt resurfaced – but not enough to make any real difference.

'You have my passport?' she asked.

'I do indeed, my little lamb.'

'And you have yours?'

'Absolutely.' He smiled, frowned, quickly checked his jacket pocket and smiled again.

'Then we must go to the British Embassy without delay and apply for a British passport for me.'

'That might be problematic,' he said.

'But I am married to a British citizen.'

'Ex,' he said.

'Ex?'

'I have just paid a visit to the Ministry of the Interior with my passport, your passport and our wedding certificate. I have renounced my British citizenship and am now a citizen of your own beloved country.'

'But I thought we were going to live in Finsbury Park?'

'That too might be problematic.'

'Huh?'

'Due to some slight misunderstanding with the authorities there, if I tried to return to Britain, I should probably be arrested at Heathrow. Or Gatwick. Or Luton. Or any other port of entry. Fortunately my new country apparently has no extradition treaty with the United Kingdom – at least, it doesn't allow its own citizens to be extradited – so I am unlikely to return to London on anything other than a purely voluntary basis. That is to say, not in the foreseeable future.'

He placed her passport on the table and his own. Though but an hour old, the cover of his new passport had already begun to curl at the edges. The heraldic eagle, picked out in gold on the sickly green surface, looked sad and dejected.

'I'm leaving you,' she said.

'That would be a shame,' he said.

'It would be what you deserve.'

'It would be a dull life if we got no more than we deserved,' he said. 'Anyway, maybe you should listen to my plan first.'

'Your plan?'

'Well, it's a bit Carlos's plan too. Did I say what a clever lad he is? Anyway, it turns out that there's some land going dead cheap out by the estuary – palm trees, golden sands, the whole works. I've got enough cash to buy it. Then we'll sell plots, maybe for just a little bit more than we paid, to the sort of people who live in Notting Hill and Hampstead, so they can build their dream homes in the sun.'

'I know where you mean. The land floods between August and October. You couldn't build anything. That's why it's cheap.'

'They won't know that in Notting Hill, though, will they?'

'They'll want to come out and see it.'

'So they can – between November and July.'

'You'd need contacts to set the deal up here.'

'I'll handle the punters from the UK. They'll trust me. They usually do for some unknown reason. Carlos understands who needs bribing at the town hall. Did I say what a clever . . .'

'Yes, you did. And how much do you reckon you'll make on it?'

'We thought we'd clear a million after our expenses.'

'Pesos?'

'Pounds.'

'Your misunderstanding with the authorities in the UK – did it have anything to do with selling land that flooded?'

He looked deeply insulted. 'The Ritz Hotel,' he said, 'never floods. Anyway, what I asked for it was a fraction of its true value. If anyone should be feeling guilty, it's the purchasers, not me.'

She took his arm affectionately. 'I think,' she said, 'that we should move somewhere cheaper than this. This hotel is lovely, but we'll need all of the cash you have in case Carlos can't get the land as cheaply as he thinks or the town hall officials are greedier than expected. Carlos isn't actually not that bright, as you'll discover. But fortunately I do know who owns the land out by the estuary, and I also know one or two things about him that his wife would find distressing if she knew too. If I pay him a visit, I'm sure he'll remember me. He'll probably be reasonable about the price when I explain things to him properly.'

'So, it's back to the Casa Blanca?'

'For a day or two until I can find us a little flat somewhere.'

'I'll check out and pay the bill then?' he said.

She surveyed the range of cheap clothing scattered over the floor. It would be a shame about the wedding dress, but it was unlikely she'd need it again.

'Unless you want any of that stuff, I think we might as well leave quietly via the back door,' she said.

'My thoughts exactly, lambkin,' he said. 'It's the only way to leave in my experience.'

THE TRAIN
Dan Waddell

Dan Waddell was born in West Yorkshire and later moved to London, where he worked as a journalist. He published non-fiction books before focusing on crime with *The Blood Detective* and *Blood Atonement.*

I check my watch and see I'm running late. Oh, the irony in that. This day, this hour, this minute, this second that I have been looking forward to like none ever before, which has absorbed every waking thought, set my heart beating so hard I feared it would hammer through my chest, the time of your return, the day you're coming back, and here I am behind schedule. It was a phone call from the office. One lousy day without me and they struggle to cope. All my working life I've given them. For what? For nothing. They couldn't give a crap. They know the year I've had and there's been no sympathy whatsoever. If I don't get a rise this year they can shove it.

Yet nothing, absolutely nothing, can alter my mood on this day of all days, not even the office. I put on my coat and scarf. The sky outside was the colour of dull aluminium when I checked earlier, after all that morning rain, and the wind whipped around the street corners in great icy blasts. But as I step out the front door and make my way down the path the sun is breaking through. It seems right, the fact it's brightening up. I can't have you coming home on such a dreary, rainy day.

I walk, half skip even, down to the end of the street, towards the station, and I'm reminded I'm late once more by the kids leaving primary school. It must be quarter past. The train arrives in five minutes. I have a quick look to see if I can see the girls. Your mother is collecting them today. She's such a saint. She takes them whenever she can. I know she's been worried, and is baffled, you just need to look at her to see that, but she says nothing and Ella and Georgie love spending time with her.

They won't believe you're coming home. And you won't believe how much they have changed. Ella is you; she has your face. Everyone comments on it. 'She looks like her mum, doesn't she?' they say, though some button-up straight afterwards. Then they give me that misty-eyed, pitying look I hate. I always knew you'd come back, you see. I'm not sure some of them did. As for Georgie, everyone says there's more of me in her. She's got my temper, I'll say that. Very wilful but that will stand her in good stead in later life.

I didn't see the girls and I couldn't stand around to see. The train will be leaving Copthorpe now, unless my watch is wrong. Just a few more minutes . . .

There's been so many changes since you went away. I built the extension you always wanted, a nice conservatory that will be lovely in the summer. George Henry and his lads did the work. He's a good bloke, George. His son Gary works with him now. Good little worker though, even though he's not all there. He kept asking me where you had gone. I don't know how many times I must have told him but he must keep forgetting. Still lives at home at thirty-one. Poor George. Though saying that he still needs to come back and finish off the patio like he promised.

Can you believe it's been a year, give or take a day or two? To contrast that dark January day, with you holding my hand in Joe's Cafe and telling me you needed to leave, with this sunny winter's afternoon. I still remember that day vividly. How could I forget? I walked away from the cafe after you said you were leaving and I was in a daze. The world kept spinning, and the sun went down, but it didn't feel like things would ever be the same.

And I was right, they weren't. Not for a long time. People would stop and make small talk, offer a kind hello, or I'd meet Jack for a pint, or there would be a good programme to watch on the TV and for a few fleeting seconds I would forget, but then reality would return and so did the knowledge I wasn't over you and wouldn't be for a while. By burying myself in work and caring for the girls, it got so that days would pass with no empty feelings. Then I'd remember you were gone and I was plunged back into the darkness, like a reset button someone kept pressing. Some friends – Dave and Clare, you remember them? – even tried to set me up with a friend of theirs! I couldn't think of anything worse. How could anyone compare to you? I know, maybe the things you said about me weren't fair, but it doesn't mean you didn't have a point. I needed to change.

When we went for a pint the other week, Jack asked me whether, if I could live my life over, given what I'd been through, would I have changed anything? Would I have married you knowing what was going to happen? I said yes, without any hesitation. If I knew then what I know now I would still be here. I was in love. Proper love. Some people never get to experience that. All the hurt, the heartbreak; it was worth it, silly as it sounds. Even in those grim days when I thought you'd never return, I never regretted meeting you. Anyway, you're coming home now, so what does all that matter?

As you can see, there's so many things to say. So many thoughts careering through my mind. I know one thing though: this time around you *will* want to stay. I promise you that, because I've had so many nights to find the way to say the right things this time, and react the way you want, and not fall into those old habits, where you feel I didn't listen, or I was too quick to get cross, or had no time for the children.

I can see the station ahead, a few more steps and I'll be there. Pretty soon I'll hold you in my arms. It's been so long since I held you. It's going to be so different. I want to talk about what you said. You know, the part of you that you said I never understood. I want to understand. I want to protect you, take good care of you, and not hurt you. It's going to be like we've started again. We're going to look so much in love to people passing by that they'll think we've just met. I might even see if your mum will take the girls and we can get away for a few days, just the two of us. But that can wait a bit, perhaps.

The bell just rang and the level crossing has started to lower. I'm on the platform and there's a few other people milling about, waiting to get on the train. Can't see anyone we know, though.

I tried to write to you. Attempted to get down some of the thoughts churning in my mind. Get across to you how sorry I was and how things would be different, how I wanted to draw a line under the past and forget the old mistakes. You know words aren't my strong point but you'd be surprised; I wrote those sort of things many, many times, but the letters just stayed inside my drawer. I kept missing the morning collection, or I'd forget to post them. When we get back, later on, when we've gone to get the kids and you've had a chance to speak with your mother, perhaps I can show you them? It might be better in a way than talking, because you know how I can stick my foot in my mouth sometimes and say the wrong thing.

There you are! In the distance I can see the train working its way round the bend by the rapeseed fields. The passengers waiting to get on move closer to the platform edge. My hands are slicked with sweat and my mouth is desert dry. It's hard for me to comprehend that you're really coming back. I look to one side and see the cars queuing either side of the crossing gate. The train has been held by a signal. I don't think I can take any more delay. The sun has disappeared once more and it's got colder. Good job I layered up.

But now the train is off again, just as I feel the first mist of drizzle on my face. It pulls in slowly, the faces in the window a blur as they pass by. I'm at the nearest platform's end, so I can see everyone get off. It comes to a halt and immediately the people waiting open the door and try and jump on before you've even got off. No manners, some people. Doors shut with a slam. I see the guard disembark. Soon he has his whistle in his mouth. A short blast. All the doors are closed now. I can't see anyone. No one got off. Maybe there was one lady but it wasn't you. Was it? I feel sure I'd recognize your face.

The train has gone and the platform is deserted. That's just weird. Did you miss the three o'clock? That must be it. You missed it. You could have phoned! I might as well wait here.

What's one hour when you've been waiting a whole year? Punctuality was never your strong point, either. That used to cause a few disagreements. Us always being late and you know how much I hate being late. It's just rude. I'll change in some ways but there're a few other principles I must adhere to. This time I'll let it go, though. Getting the train and coming back here can't have been that easy when you've been gone a while, and you're returning to a small place where everyone knows each other's business, which means that they would know you were prepared to walk out on your husband and your two kids on the spurious basis that your life wasn't working out the way you wanted it to. You see, they don't know you wanted to take the girls. They think you abandoned them and they're a conservative bunch round here and they think that's just unnatural, a mum leaving her little ones behind while she goes and gads about. There were times when I was going to tell people the truth. Hundreds of times! Sometimes the urge to speak the truth was overwhelming, but I always thought of the girls and what was best for them.

I step under the platform awning for a bit of shelter. A few gentlemen appear on the platform. That's a bit strange as I don't think there's another train going west for at least half an hour and this is no place to wait in this weather. They're wearing suits. Probably been here on some business at the industrial park on the edge of the village and on their way back to the town.

They're coming this way. Probably going to ask me when the next train is. There's never anyone in the ticket office, I tell you. They're going to be a bit ticked off when I say they've just missed one. Come to think of it, they looked pretty hacked off anyway. Faces all serious and concerned, looking over their shoulder. There's a few more people behind them too. Policemen, of all people. Oh no. Don't tell me some daft bugger has gone and thrown themselves under a train.

The older one, in a Macintosh, has got a thin, mirthless smile on his face. The other, a younger man, looks a bit nervous. Those officers are running now. This looks serious.

Yes, that's my name, I say, when the one in the mac asks. He says something. I don't hear. The wind carries it a bit.

Say that again, I ask. He wants me to come with them. Nice and quiet, he says. No need to do anything sudden or stupid. Apparently they've found a woman's body.

Just then, the rain gets heavier.

MASKS FOR EVERY OCCASION
Yvonne Walus

Yvonne Walus was born and raised in Poland; later her family moved to South Africa. She now lives in New Zealand and is a Doctor of Mathematics who works as a business analyst. In addition to articles, short stories and poetry, she has published novels in various genres, sometimes under a pseudonym.

11 June, 2010

The journalist from the far-flung idyll of England was the first victim.

'A burglary gone wrong,' Captain de Vos dismissed the murder. 'It's a shame it had to happen to a tourist, though. Speak to the hotel security and wrap it up.' He changed his mask of a dutiful policeman to that of a soccer fan. 'Wouldn't want to miss the kick-off.'

His error was understandable given the crime statistics in South Africa.

It never occurred to de Vos to engage my services as a crime profiler, even though we work together by day and sleep together most nights. The sleeping together would have put us in jail a mere two decades ago, for de Vos is as white as an elephant tusk and I'm the black of the triangle in our flag. The apartheid-day taboo still thrills me, though.

That historic June afternoon, the country shut early. De Vos and I watched the broadcast of the FIFA World Cup opening match together. With all five of my brothers soccer players, and one of them a reserve in this competition, my heart and soul may as well have been the Jabulani ball.

Hypnotized by the beehive hum of the vuvuzelas emitting from the TV set and the calming rhythm of the game, I slipped into bliss-out. Even my headache subsided.

THWACK!

The first goal shook the entire stadium, eighty thousand throats exploding in primordial cries of triumph. My pride swelled like the Limpopo in the rainy season. De Vos jumped off the sofa and punched the air, freedom-fighter style.

'Yes!' He jerked me towards him and twirled us across the floor. 'We may be ranked eighty-third, but we play mean soccer.'

A complex reaction from a man ready to desert his land for the much greener grass of the British Isles. I searched his face for the mask of a patriot or a traitor, but saw only a boy supporting his team.

When we settled down, I snuggled into his embrace. 'You know the journalist killed earlier today?'

'The Englishman?' De Vos didn't move his eyes away from the screen. 'It hasn't hit the news yet. They don't want it to spoil the moment. Why?'

'He was here to comment on the World Cup.' I pulled the laptop towards us. 'I'll show you the last article he wrote for his newspaper. No, that's not the one.' I clicked away from the guy's satire on rape and found the right article, a tongue-in-cheek exposé titled, 'Soccer Increasingly Boring Because Losing No Longer a Capital Offence'.

'Ironic,' said de Vos.

Sacrilegious, I thought.

My personal blog that night didn't mention the murder, though I did mention the journalist and scathe his lack of respect for soccer. By morning, my entry had acquired an anonymous comment. *'The journalist deserved to die. Look for the offender's signature: it's more idiosyncratic than the modus operandi.'*

17 June, 2010

The rapist's face wore polite boredom like a tribal mask. I swallowed the urge to ram my BlackBerry down his throat. Across the desk from me sat the sleazeball who'd forced at least three tourists at knifepoint as they were leaving Soccer City after late-night games. My profiling had identified him. All I had to do now was prove his guilt.

'Are you free for dinner tonight?' His words drilled into my head, sick-stations sweet. 'We could watch the soccer. You're a fascinating woman, Dr . . .' He squinted at my nametag. 'Dr Elizabeth Mphela. I've never known a crime profiler before. What was your PhD topic?'

I knew better than to answer, so I was surprised to hear my voice. 'Multiple identity disorder.'

'Oh, yeah? Which of your identities wants to suck me off first?'

The phone felt slippery in my grip. *Control*, I heard deep inside me.

I concentrated on my notes, pressing every BlackBerry key with the tip of my nail slowly, poisoned by the potion of the rapist's presence.

The suspect's aggressive stance and insistent denials indicate a reluctance to see himself as a sexual offender, making medical or psychiatric treatment unfeasible.

My phone pinged. I glanced at the subject line: New Murder Last Night, Drop Everything.

Adrenaline buzzed on my tongue. 'That will be all for today, Mr Spencer. Thank you for your time. One of the detectives will escort you out.'

His grin showed too many teeth, too white and too sharp in his hairless skull shaped like a slug. 'You know you don't have enough evidence to hold me. How about that soccer date?'

God bless Africa with men like him walking free.

'We'll meet again, Mr Spencer, though not for soccer.'

Wrong as I was, it would be weeks before I realized, but for now, I busied myself with the new case.

'Hey,' I said when I arrived at the victim's hotel. 'Is this the ref who fell for the dive in yesterday's match?'

The medical examiner must have been the only person in the country not assaulted with the World Cup fever.

'Huh?' he replied. 'This is a soccer ref, Elizabeth, not a scuba diver.'

'*Yebo*, how right you are. If only more soccer players realized it.'

I checked the paperwork. The victim's name I knew straight

away. It was etched for ever into the memory of all South Africans who'd seen us lose yesterday – on Soweto Day of all days – thanks to this referee's incompetence. Fewer of my countrymen knew that the murdered man was also implicated in a sex scandal.

Serves you right, I thought as I stared at his face, hardened into a death mask.

When I got home that night, I blogged the sentiment. As the officials had put a clamp on all negative news during the Cup and the world knew nothing about the referee's demise, I phrased it as a hypothetical question: '*Who's more at fault: a soccer player who dives or a ref who falls for it?*'

The next morning, another anonymous comment loomed on my blog: '*The blame is equal.* Note: *Victimology identifies similarities between each of the victims of a particular crime to establish a definite pattern.*'

Dread took its prickly constitutional down my spine. Whoever was responding to my blog was no layman.

That should have tipped me off. It probably would have. Only, my deductive process was interrupted by a text message from my brother, the FIFA benchwarmer: I will be playing in the third match.

The red card turned out to be a blessing for one family, at least. That evening, our whole clan gathered in Soweto. We wore our happy masks, not wanting to remember the double defeat of Soweto Day, not the one in 1976 nor the FIFA one the previous day. The home-brewed sorghum beer we celebrated on didn't contain battery acid like *isikilimikwiki*, the kill-me-quickly some people make; nevertheless, I spent the whole of Saturday tending my head.

Time stretched and shrank in unrealism like a Salvador Dali painting. I slept.

27 June, 2010

South Africa fell out of the competition, despite my brother's dazzling play in the last match of the group stage. While the rest of the country swayed under the blow, I secretly harboured the hope this would herald the end of the serial killings.

Nobody else shared my optimism. They were right.

The third victim's hotel suite belonged in a brothel, or at least in my idea of what a brothel should look like. A circular bed. A large mirror on the ceiling. Red plush chairs with gilded legs and armrests. An opened champagne bottle in an ice bucket of sludge.

This time, I got to the crime scene before de Vos.

'How long?' I asked.

'A few hours ago. Three tops. More likely under two.'

I checked the time. The victim had played in the soccer match against England earlier that afternoon. De Vos and I had travelled to Bloemfontein to watch it live, because:

one, I am a soccer addict,

two, we could claim it as a legitimate investigation cost and,

three, de Vos loves all things English. Oh, how colourfully he swore when the English equaliser was disregarded, and how loudly he stormed out of our hotel room when the match was over.

Victimology. The word echoed in my brain. My voice came out all hollow. 'This guy. He's the goalie, right?'

'The cheat who pretended the goal never happened,' de Vos's voice sounded from the door. 'Good riddance.'

I took another look around me. A perfect place to entertain soccer groupies or underage prostitutes. Judging by the multishaded lipstick stains on the champagne glasses and on the victim's skin, this room was used for that very purpose. I counted the colours. Four. Despite myself, I felt something close to impressed. I know our Zulu boys can give a girl a good time many times in one evening, but I never imagined Europeans capable of the same feat.

Take de Vos, for example . . .

'Elizabeth? You OK?'

'What?' I came back to the here and now. 'Sure.'

I went back to doing my job. Ostensibly, this was presenting like yet another burglary in which the perpetrators panic and take the crime to a higher level. It wasn't.

'The third crime scene looks identical to the previous two,' I said into my BlackBerry. Oh, the wonders of modern technology, when your phone is also your Dictaphone and web browser. I'm waiting for the day this compilation of miracles comes out as a wristwatch with 3D output. 'The victim was shot with a single bullet to the head. The MO as well as the selection of victims seems to indicate a single killer.'

Victimology.

What did the three victims have in common, apart from soccer? A journalist, a ref, a goalie, all of different nationalities. The first victim's articles may have offended a soccer fan. The second one was hated by all South Africa supporters, the third one by the English. It didn't add up, and yet I could feel it in the marrow of my bones and on the tip of my thoughts.

'By the way,' I asked as I packed up to leave the crime scene, 'where are we with our soccer fan rapist?'

De Vos shook his head.

My pulse reverberated hot against my eardrums. 'You let him go?'

'We had nothing concrete, Elizabeth. Condoms are a wonderful invention against AIDS, but they don't help the forensics.'

'Hair?' I asked desperately. Then, remembering his completely bald head, 'Body hair?'

Rape is the most reprehensible of all crimes. Murder takes only the remainder of your life. Rape robs you of your dignity, of your womanhood, of your memories and of your chances at future happiness.

In South Africa, rape is so brutal it robs you of your humanity.

De Vos shot me a look. He knew about my past, had seen the scars, and not only the ones on the inside. He knew not to give me compassion. His boyfriend mask hid under that of an investigator. 'The bastard shaves everything.' The investigator mask slipped. 'Sorry.'

Everybody working on the FIFA murder case received a stern warning not to talk to anybody outside our circle, and so my blog entry for the night consisted of a row of question marks.

That didn't stop my anonymous comment-writer. Before long, the following words appeared in the comments box: '*Every*

serial killer works to a certain set of self-imposed values, values
as unique and identifiable as handwriting.'
I couldn't have put it better myself.
Trouble was, what values?
Justice, whispered something inside my very core.

28 June, 2010

It all went conspiracy theory after that. The official account, to
explain the victims' absence from the games, was food poisoning.
It was such a good conspiracy theory, everybody bought it. Our
country is good at wearing masks suitable for every occasion.
To the overseas crowd, we only ever show the exotic.

The direct elimination matches were in full swing, the
quarter-finals looming, and the boss was pushing me to predict
the serial killer's next move.

'I need a result, Elizabeth,' he said at the special team
meeting this morning, his mask all no nonsense and no
excuses.

I may be sleeping with de Vos, he may be hoping to persuade
me to move to England with him, but at work he's still the
boss.

'Yes, Captain,' was the only appropriate reply, though I did
promise myself I'd get him back at home.

'Can you narrow the field for us?' he asked. 'Race, age,
geographical location?'

I shrugged. 'Clearly someone who won't raise suspicions
entering posh hotels. Smart enough to lay false clues. A soccer
enthusiast. Someone whom the victims would invite into their
hotel rooms.' You didn't have to be a crime profiler to come
up with any of that. 'Comfortable using a gun.' Well, that
narrowed it down. Not. Most South Africans, children and old
people included, could shoot a gun in their sleep. 'The gun is
untraceable, I take it?'

De Vos nodded, stretched, got up. 'OK, people. We have a
job to do.'

I hoped my mask said, 'Right on it, boss.' My heart sure
as hell didn't.

Back in my office, I stared at the wall. The desert-empty

whiteboard hung like an accusation next to an A1 sheet with the schedule of all the World Cup matches. With a red marker, I recorded the names of the three victims, the dates of their deaths, their professions. I didn't need to do this; good memory is in every African's genes thanks to centuries of illiteracy, but I felt better for doing it.

Next, in green and thankfully very-much-delible ink, I composed a list of suspects:

1. Disgruntled soccer fan.
2. Disgruntled player.
3. A gambler trying to improve the odds for his wager.
4. Somebody who wanted to kill only one of the victims and used the others as a smokescreen.
5. A fellow crime profiler.

Point number five chafed. I rubbed it out with the heel of my hand. Yet it was hard to argue with the facts. Back it went. No, anybody could walk in and see it. Out.

In the end, I settled for an acronym, FCP: Fellow Crime Profiler. Great. Now what?

Made fashionable by Hollywood, criminal profiling is the grey area between law enforcement science and the art of psychology. It's a relatively new field with no set methodology and few guidelines for the practitioners. I spent the rest of the day following bullet trajectories and running statistical analysis on anything that could be analysed.

'Coming to watch the game?' De Vos stood in the doorway, a six-pack balanced in the palm of his hand, his mask of choice that of a carefree boyfriend bent on NOT talking about his woman's rape.

I shrugged. 'Dunno. Who's playing?' I couldn't remember.

Funny that. With South Africa out of the Word Cup, my soccer spirit had dwindled. It was no longer a matter of patriotism to follow the sport. I would do my country a far greater service catching the serial killer.

'Come on, Elizabeth, please. It's Monday and we haven't exactly had a weekend. Your place, my beer?'

I capitulated. 'Whatever you say. You're the boss.'

Two hours later, the boss mask changed into a soccer fan. 'Cheating!' The beer can crunched, crushed by de Vos's fist.

Beer dregs ran down his elbow on to the lounge carpet. Mine. 'Did you see that? Elizabeth, did you see? What a diver. What a performer. What a fake.'

'Mmmmm.' There is something hypnotic and mesmerizing in soccer's rhythm. I was in my zone, reluctant to surface.

De Vos had found his groove. 'Doesn't he know this is South Africa? It's a dangerous country in which to get on the wrong side of the crowd.'

I said nothing.

'Elizabeth.'

'What? The ref isn't buying any of it. Just sit down, relax, enjoy the game.'

The huffy mask went on and De Vos left as soon as the first game of the day was over, ranting and raving and fuming at the alleged cheating side's victory.

Another massive headache threatened to emerge, so I went straight to bed. Before I fell asleep, I blogged a few disjointed lines on the topic of, '*It's the coach's fault anyway for letting them fake injuries*'. The pain got worse.

I was jerked awake by a phone call from de Vos. 'We have another one.'

My head still hurt. Even before he said it, though, I knew. I let him say it anyway. 'The coach.'

'I'll be right there. Which hotel?'

Despite my promise, I didn't leave straight away. The laptop took for ever to boot up. The ISP dropped me three times before I got to my blog page.

The anonymous comment, left three hours earlier, read: '*According to Turvey, behavioural analysis is not effective in practice. Not only do criminals think differently than most people, but their behaviour has different meanings in different cultures. In some countries, rape is an acceptable way of life.*'

There was no escaping it. Brent Turvey, the authority on forensic science. The serial killer was one of us.

6 July, 2010

Bribery is most resplendent on Africa's soil, cracked and ridden with parasites like elephant hide. Despite the international flavour of the murders, the facts slipped away unnoticed by the media. No uproar, no scandal, not even a mention.

A voice in my head said it was a good thing. My boyfriend, wearing the boss mask, said I had a job to do. I listened to both.

And I speculated.

Predominantly, serial killers come from dysfunctional families or suffer a trauma in their formative years. They are almost always assumed to be men, and that's true when the murders go hand in hand with sexual assault on the victim. Black Widows and Angels of Death, though, are predominantly women. While male serial killers kill for sexual reasons, female ones typically kill for profit.

The FIFA murders didn't fit the bill.

Crime profiling methods had proved useless. The serial killer was too good. I resorted to some good old-fashioned sleuthing.

'Has anybody reviewed any of the hotels' security tapes?' I asked de Vos.

'Er.' He sent me a charming grin. 'At least we reviewed a lot of soccer footage?'

I appropriated his computer and settled for a day of boredom. Given the choice between watching security tapes and watching paint dry, I'd go for the latter. Watching paint dry is easier on the eyes.

De Vos had already done all the grunge work of selecting the recordings taken around the times of the murders, so I was spared having to fast forward through hours of irrelevant copy.

I recognized the leather jacket on the footage of the first murder, but it took me two more to realize what I was seeing. Every time, the leather jacket had arrived at the hotel *before* the body was discovered.

This was not happening. A round, hard ball of foreboding lodged in my throat. Slowly, every shift forward an effort, I walked towards the closet where we kept our coats and gloves in winter, when the African mornings are cold enough to go sub-zero.

The mossy green of the leather peeked from behind my red woollen poncho and de Vos's duffle coat. Inside the right-hand pocket of the jacket, my hand encountered the familiar shape of metal death.

No hesitation, no second thoughts, no guilty conscience. I began by hard-erasing the footage from de Vos's computer. Nobody was likely to miss it for the moment, and I made a mental note to return with a strong magnet to complete the job. Task one, check.

Task two. 'Captain?' I said in my best professional voice. 'Would a specialist be able to trace an anonymous comment placed on a blog?'

'Theoretically. You need the blog owner's permission, or you have to serve a court order on their ISP provider to get the data. Why? Do we have something?'

His anticipation mask was almost heartbreaking. Almost.

'No, sorry. It was just a random thought. I wanted to give hell to the FIFA officials for not coming down harder on all the cheating. Where is the sportsmanship in soccer? The cheats actually gloat about it in the media afterwards.'

Task three, delete those comments. Make that, delete the whole blog.

'Your brother played brilliant soccer, though,' de Vos said, his hand briefly on my shoulder. 'He'll make them eat dirt in Brazil.'

I gave him an empty nod. The next World Cup seemed light years away.

Now for task four. I'm not proud of what I did next. Yet I did it – I, Elizabeth Mphela, PhD in Multiple Identity Disorders. Nobody else. I take full responsibility.

Funny thing, though, human conscience. Mine didn't bother me one bit as I pleaded a headache to de Vos and told him to watch the soccer without me.

This time, I didn't have a headache. I arrived at my destination just before the kick-off. Neither of the semi-final matches was held at Soccer City, so I was sure the Soccer City Rapist would be home.

'Hello, Mr Spencer,' I said to the camera at his gate. Task five, destroy this footage when I'm done. 'I've come to take you up on your dinner invitation.'

The fool let me in. You should have seen his mask.

It was child's play to shoot him with the same gun as those used by the serial killer, the one I found in the jacket pocket.

Live by the sword, die by the sword. No remorse. Thanks to my training, I knew exactly where to aim it to make it look like suicide.

I used his computer to send his confession to the general police email address available on the web. Then I watched the game on his home entertainment centre. The cheating team lost the semi-final. Justice prevailed.

It was me, my own identity, all the time. No headache, no time distortion, no memory loss.

What I'd loved most about my doctoral thesis was the controversy surrounding the existence of the multiple identity disorder. Now I loved the irony. Multiple identities, masks for every occasion. I had perfected the concept.

My BlackBerry rang. I checked the caller ID. De Vos, the man with many masks yet only one identity.

'Elizabeth. How's your head?'

'Good.'

'Will you marry me?' Through the miles that separated us, I could hear he was wearing his mask of a drunk.

I thought about it. 'Do we have to emigrate?'

'Probably. Is that a problem? The English are bloody good at soccer, you know.'

South Africa, my country, from the cradle to the grave. The last thing I wanted was to leave my roots. But I had masks of my own to bury, and faraway seemed like a good place for the funeral. 'OK.'

Besides, England already hosted the World Cup back in 1966. The chances of them bagging another one any time soon were practically zilch.

My alter ego would be safe there . . .